Ghosts of Grady

GRADY LAKE MYSTERY SERIES
BOOK THREE

JL HYDE

Other Titles by J. L. Hyde:

Underground

Delta County

Summer of '99

Midnight in Delta County

Magnolia Court

Grady Lake

Secrets of Grady

First paperback edition July 2024

Cover Design by Allsweet Studios and Brandon Kobs

ISBN 979-8-9871631-4-6 (Paperback)

www.jlhyde.com

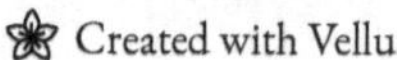 Created with Vellum

*To the readers of BookTok and Bookstagram, who make me feel
like we're all in this together:*

This one's for you.

Once you eliminate the impossible, whatever remains, no matter how improbable, must be the truth.

-Arthur Conan Doyle

Prologue

IN BOOK TWO, *Secrets of Grady*, we saw Malorie Rose Benard return home after twenty years in captivity. Her family, the Benards, struggled to welcome back a loved one who was not the same girl they had lost in 2003. Through a little therapy and a lot of patience, Malorie began to come out of her room and communicate her feelings, improving a little more each day.

Sammie Spencer, Lincoln Palmer's final kidnapping victim, returned to Grady Lake to give an interview about her ordeal to Nolan for his podcast, *Gone, but Not Forgotten*. When Sammie doesn't show up for the interview, everyone assumes she got cold feet . . . until her body is recovered from a small cove near the shoreline the next day. Her death is quickly ruled an accident because she was found tangled in the bramble below the surface of the shallow water, and several eyewitnesses reported seeing her wandering by the lake alone, taking photographs of the freshly fallen snow.

Through a series of flashbacks, we learn that Lincoln Palmer manipulated Rich Lowery into using his land for an underground marijuana growing operation. Shortly after building underground bunkers, Rich finds out that Lincoln isn't growing illegal drugs—he's kidnapping and possibly murdering teenage girls. We know Rich recognizes an accomplice of Palmer's, who shows up several times in the early years on Rich's trail cameras aimed at the bunkers. Rich is relieved that he hasn't seen the man on his property in years, so he's convinced his old friend has come to his senses and no longer associates with Palmer and his dirty deeds. During the flashbacks, we see the man flicking an engraved silver lighter open and closed . . . the lighter he received as a gift for standing in Rich's wedding years ago. By the end of the book, we know both Sheriff Nelson *and* Charles David (Malorie and Katie's dad) own these lighters.

The sad truth about the death of the girls' mother, Beth Benard, is revealed. Though she did not die of a heart attack on the trail between the lodge and the Grab N Go, there is some relief in knowing that she died knowing Malorie was still alive. Beth didn't go to her grave wondering who took her daughter; she knew it was her old friend Rich, who incorrectly assumed Malorie was his biological daughter.

A romantic relationship begins between our main character, Katie, and Nolan, the podcaster who helped find her sister. We even see a possible flirtation between Aunt Lou and Lieutenant Robert Barkley, who is in town for the investigations.

At the end of *Secrets of Grady*, we learn three bombshells: Nicole (Katie's best friend) saw Malorie in her father's basement, the baby Mal was told died during childbirth is alive and well (and it's Robbie, who works on the docks), and a chest full of USB drives with camera footage from the bunkers is found . . . and may have incriminating footage of Sheriff

Nelson. Oh, and Lincoln Palmer's other mystery accomplice is Chelsey, the Benard's newest employee . . . and Cousin Dougie's new love interest.

Welcome to the third and final book in the Grady Lake Mystery Series.

One

SURELY, I've misheard the words that just came out of my sister's mouth. I swear she just accused my best friend of knowing she was kept in her father's basement.

In the words of my Aunt Lou, "Nicole isn't *just* my best friend; Nicole is family." She is one of us. She cried alongside us for twenty years while we mourned the loss of Malorie, who we were certain was gone forever. Our lives were never the same. You're telling me Nicole not only knew my sister was in her father's basement, but she didn't save her or tell anyone? Not possible. It's just not possible.

"I know you don't owe me a thing, but I'm asking you to please listen to me," Nicole says, barely above a whisper, her voice shaking.

"You have two minutes to explain yourself before I go out there and tell Katie. I've waited long enough for you to come clean. She needs to know who her best friend really is," Malorie says in a voice so cold I barely recognize it as coming from my only sister.

I can't take it, and against my better judgement I burst into the room and tightly close the door behind me. Malorie's eyes widen and she stumbles backward slightly. I just over-heard a conversation I was never meant to know about. Nicole is frozen, redness crawling up her neck and is inhaling sharply with ragged breaths. She collapses onto my bed and leans forward, elbows on her knees and head hung in shame.

"Nicole you're a lot of things, but I've never known you to be a liar. That's why I'm certain that whatever is about to come out of your mouth will be an accurate explanation of why my sister seems to think you saw her in that basement."

Tears aren't just trickling down her cheeks; they are pouring out of her eyes, landing in small pools on the hard-wood floor beneath her. Other than rapidly sniffing and attempting to catch her breath, she isn't making a sound. Nicole has never lied to me. She can't start now.

"Do you remember the night the *Benzo Chronicles* stopped being funny?" she says, eyes still fixed on the floor until they slowly rise to meet mine when I don't immediately respond.

Sometime in the early years after I left for college, Nicole began having issues sleeping at night, mostly due to anxiety. When it became such an issue that Mae caught her dozing off during a shift at the Grab N Go, she made Nicole an appoint-ment with her primary care doctor in Marquette. Rather than doing any tests or asking questions to get to the bottom of her sudden sleep struggles and increased anxiety, he handed her a prescription for a generic benzodiazepine and sent her on her way.

At first, it was like a miracle drug. Nicole didn't have a care in the world. She began sleeping eight or nine hours a night. It came with a price, though. Nicole would wake up in the guest room of her apartment; sometimes a jar of peanut butter would be found open on the counter, with no recollection of how it got there. She'd log onto AOL Instant Messenger and have lengthy conversations with old friends, not remembering a word of it in the morning. She often called me in the middle of the night, resulting in rambling three-minute voicemails. We were in our early twenties; we thought it was hilarious. Quickly dubbed the *Benzo Chronicles*, I lived for the updates she'd give me on my morning walk to class. I hung on every word until I reached my building and had to end the call. Each story was increasingly absurd—doing loads of laundry, washing dishes, even opening and drinking a bottle of beer in her sleep. Nicole had never been a sleepwalker; yet, this medicine had her performing entire chore lists with no recollection of them whatsoever the next morning. It was funny, until it wasn't.

One morning, she didn't answer my call. In fact, she didn't return my calls for days. When I finally got ahold of her by dialing the store directly during one of her shifts, she was short with me. Evasive. Dodgy. She promised she'd call me later when she could talk in private. When she called that night, it was anything but funny. She was incredibly vague about the details, but she told me that the prescribed drug had become too much, and she was going to have to find another way to sleep. The only hint she gave me of what had transpired was that she had a horrible hallucination and it scared her enough to quit cold turkey. Hearing the seriousness of her tone terrified me. I offered to drive home to Grady, but she declined. We never talked about it again.

"Dad and Mae started worrying about me when I was eating and drinking in my sleep. They were convinced I was going to choke on something. I started sleeping over at Mae's until I could ween myself off the meds, but I needed them. I couldn't quit. She had an overnight trip planned to Green Bay with some of the ladies from Bingo, so I agreed to stay at Dad's for the night so he could keep an eye on me."

My eyes dart over to Mal, who is now sitting on the edge of her bed, eyes glistening. She was there, in the basement.

Rich let Nicole stay over at his cabin while my sister was held hostage just beneath her feet. It's unfathomable.

"When I woke up the next morning, it wasn't like a normal morning after a benzo sleep. I was in full panic mode. I was convinced I saw Malorie. Dad did his best to calm me down and called Dr. Irving in front of me. He asked if hallucinations could be a side effect of taking the drug nightly, and he kept nodding as Irving spoke. Now I wonder if he called him at all. He drove me home after breakfast, but I couldn't shake the feeling. It felt so real. I swore I had seen her."

My eyes haven't left Malorie's. I know Nicole well enough to know she's telling this story exactly as she remembers it, but Mal hasn't known her since she was a teenager. She doesn't know the woman Nicole grew up to be—the best friend I'd trust with my life.

"Later that day, Dad and I went fishing, and I confided in him how real the vision was and how I had a clear memory of lifting the trap door and wandering down the wooden stairs to his basement and opening his doomsday room, looking for peanut butter. I was always eating peanut butter on the benzos, and I knew he kept cases of it in storage. I looked in the room, but in my vision, it wasn't a storage room anymore; it was a bedroom. There was a girl sleeping in a bed in the corner, and when she opened her eyes, I knew it was Malorie. She was pale and had much shorter hair, but I was sure it was her. I closed the door and walked back up the stairs, willing myself to wake up from the nightmare. I was crying and slapping myself in the face so I'd wake up. Dad heard me crying and came out to give me something that would help me go back to sleep and I did—I passed out cold."

Nicole turns her gaze to Malorie, who isn't showing any emotion at all. She's allowing Nicole to speak, which is more than a lot of people would be allowing in a moment like this.

"He told me that if I was so upset by my dream, maybe I

should go back to his house and check out the storage room for myself and see that there's nobody in there. That's exactly what we did; we packed up our tackle boxes, threw them in the truck, and he drove me straight to the cabin. He opened the wooden door, motioned for me to go down, and he was right—you weren't there. It was just a storage room, just like I had seen a thousand times. I swear, Malorie. You weren't there. When you were rescued, I kept waiting for you to confront me about it, and when you didn't, that made up my mind that I really did hallucinate that night from the drugs."

"He moved me for a full week because he knew you saw me. He kept me in the dark for days," Mal says, shaking her head to rid her mind of the memory.

"Where did he take you?" I ask.

"At the time, I had no idea. Now I think it must have been one of the bunkers on his land. It was definitely underground."

"Malorie, you have to believe me. He had me convinced I imagined it all. It scared me so much, I quit taking the meds that day. I don't think I slept for more than an hour at a time for weeks."

Mal's eyes quickly dart to mine before locking in an intense gaze, silently asking me if I believe Nicole.

"When was your first hint that what you saw might have been real? When did you know?" I ask Nicole.

"The Polaroid that Khaki Pants found in Dad's basement. Her hair was short . . . exactly like my vision of her. At that moment, I realized either benzos had given me psychic visions, or it really was Mal that I saw all those years ago. Then it was the one-two punch of realizing my dad was responsible and that Mae took part in it; so, to be honest, I haven't had much time for it to register. I really did see Mal in my dad's basement, and that asshole gaslit me into believing I had hallucinated it all."

I look back at Mal, giving her the slightest nod to signify that I do, against all odds, absolutely believe what Nicole is telling us. Not only because she's always been honest, but because there's no way she could come up with such a believable back story on her own.

"We can work through this, Nicole. I think it's just going to take some time," Mal tells her. Her hand twitches, and I know she wants to reach forward and squeeze Nicole's hand or pat her shoulder, but she isn't quite ready yet.

Commotion in the hallway outside our room steals our attention from the conversation. I throw the door open and rush in the direction of all the noise—Dougie's room. All three aunts are huddled around him as he vomits into a small trash can next to his bed. Judging by the mess, the trash can wasn't available when he began getting sick.

I know he had a few too many drinks last night, but Dougie is a professional drinker. He can hold his liquor as well as men twice his size. I'm not sure I've ever seen him so hungover that he's physically ill, and certainly not in bad enough shape to lose it before he can make it to the bathroom.

"Maybe it was something he ate?" Aunt Brenda suggests. Her maternal love for her son takes precedence over logic.

"We all ate at The Moose Trap and nobody else is sick," Aunt Deb points out.

The aunts fuss over Dougie with damp wash cloths, Pepto Bismol, and cans of ginger ale while the rest of the family backs out of the room to give him some space. I stay in the doorway for a moment, taking in his condition. His skin is a sickly shade of gray with his bloodshot eyes barely opening when someone speaks to him.

They mindlessly list each dish that was served at my birthday party last night, measuring the hypothetical risks of foodborne illness for each, while I replay the interactions I had with Dougie's new fling, Chelsey. She refused to let him go home with Nolan and me. She locked eyes with me while she kissed him. She made several questionable quips in my direction throughout the night. She remained curiously sober. It may be because I've been recently devastated by the actions of several people whom I've known for most of my life, but I'm certainly paying close attention to this woman, who inserted herself in our lives only a week ago. I've been fooled enough; I will not be fooled again, especially when it comes to the well-being of my family.

BACK IN THE family room of the lodge, everyone pitches in to clean up after the gathering—even Sheriff Nelson and Robbie. It's another thing I love about small towns—it's not even a discussion; everyone just begins to help when the event is over.

Nolan is gathering the last of the discarded wrapping paper from my gifts as I perform my best attempt at pretending the interaction with Nicole and Malorie never happened. Lately, I've gotten comfortable telling Nolan just about everything that's on my mind, but this is a secret I'll be keeping inside our circle of three for a while. I believe every word Nicole said, but it doesn't make it any less unsettling. She saw my sister. She saw the woman the entire nation was searching for, and it was in her own father's basement. This isn't going to be a one-and-done conversation.

Malorie has perfectly acclimated herself into the role of teasing Robbie for his misdemeanor arrest; and Nicole, who normally would be leading the mission, is quietly sweeping confetti from the kitchen floor. Lou is cussing at Nelson for putting away dishes in the wrong cupboards, and Karli is leaned back on the kitchen island, getting a kick out of the show. I'm startled when a large hand is placed on my shoulder, and I spin to see it's just my dad.

"Where did you go?" I ask, realizing I haven't seen him in at least thirty minutes.

"I don't do so well with the puking; I had to step outside and get some fresh air," he says, gesturing to Dougie's room.

"Ahh, that must be why you disappeared so much when we were young, eh?" I tease.

He playfully rubs his knuckles on the top of my head before pulling me into an embrace.

"You get that smart mouth from your mother; have I ever told you that?" he says with a smile before kissing my forehead. "All joking aside, I've gotta get back to Marquette. I hope you have the best birthday there ever was, Katie Bug."

"Other than *your* nephew projectile vomiting across the hall from my bedroom, it's been a pretty good morning. Love you, Dad."

He hugs Mal and says his goodbyes to the rest of the family, avoiding Dougie's room but shouting his wishes for a speedy recovery on his way out, while Brenda throws her son's soiled sheets in a trash bag to be brought downstairs. We won't be letting Dougie live this down anytime soon.

Sheriff Nelson steps out on the patio to take a call, and his jovial off-day mood has dissipated when he steps back in. "I've got to get down to the station. Enjoy the rest of your birthday, Katie," he mumbles to me on his way out.

"Wonder what that's about?" Deb asks after we hear Nelson's footsteps descend the stairs.

As I look around the room, it's uncanny how well I can read each of their thoughts. Deb and Brenda are concerned, not only for Nelson but for whoever is requiring the assistance of Grady's sheriff on his only day off. Lou is wondering how she can step into action and help the situation. Malorie is worried it's another girl, and so is Nicole, but for different reasons. I don't think she can stomach anymore heartache being attributed to her father. There's no doubt in my mind that Nolan and Karli are dying to know what Nelson got called back to the station for. If it's in any way related to Mal's case, they will be chomping at the bit to get the scoop before any other journalists. Sweet, sweet Robbie is simply sitting on the couch, eating his second plate of breakfast, and watching a sitcom rerun on TV, clearly oblivious to any of the activity around him.

"The nineteen hundreds had the best shows, I swear," Robbie says to nobody in particular. You can practically hear the record screeching to a halt as we all stop what we're doing and turn in his direction. He's watching *King of Queens.*

"What the *hell* did you just say?" Nicole asks, walking in his direction.

Robbie's eyes dart from Nicole to me and back again. We've already established how horrible he is at reading a room, and Nicole always has to spell it out for him when she's joking.

"The . . . ahh . . . the guide says this show came out in 1998. Is that wrong?" he asks, setting his plate in his lap and clicking the guide button on the remote, as if we are looking for proof.

"If you ever refer to 1998 as the nineteen hundreds again, I'm throwing your scrawny ass in that lake, Robbie," Nicole tells him. "I'd slap you, but then you'd drop your plate of pancakes, and Lou would kill me in my sleep tonight for staining the carpet."

Nicole still hasn't cracked a smile, so Robbie's gaze shoots over to Lou. She nods in confirmation. Mal is the first to lose it, spitting out her drink when she can't hold the laughter in anymore.

"I've been locked in a basement for the last twenty years, so I don't know many people in your generation, but you're not giving me a good first impression, kid," Mal tells him, patting him on the shoulder from her standing position behind the couch.

"They're called Gen Z, and spoiler alert—they all suck," Nicole replies directly to Malorie but is still too wounded to look her in the eye.

"You guys suck," Robbie replies, barely audible. Surely after a full season with us, he'll get sharper with the comebacks.

Mal nods to Nicole before returning to the kitchen to help with clean up. It's the closest Nicole is going to get to receiving forgiveness today, and the way she exhales after Mal walks away says it's all she needs.

Anyone listening to Nicole describe how she was convinced that she simply dreamed up seeing a kidnapped woman in her father's basement would be shaking their heads in disbelief. I, however, believe every word she told us and can only pray that Malorie does, too.

Three

LATER THAT NIGHT, I'm walking the path from the lodge to Nolan's cabin when I spot Karli leaving. Once I'm within twenty feet or so, I realize she's crying, so I hurry my pace, calling out her name.

"Oh, hey Katie. I was just leaving. He's in there editing," she tells me, gesturing to the cabin door with one hand and quickly wiping under her eyes with the other.

"How can I help?" I ask her. It's a little trick I overheard Dalia, Mal's therapist, discussing with the aunts last week. It's more likely to be well received than, "why are you crying?" or "what's wrong?" and gets the person you're talking to focused on a solution, rather than the issue itself.

"I'm not going to bore you with my sob story on your birthday. I'll be just fine," she says, doing a horrible job of downplaying the situation. Now that I'm standing in front of her, I can see the dry, inflamed skin around her nose and expect to find a trash can full of discarded tissues when I get inside the cabin.

"I can't force you to talk to me about it, but I'll remind you that I'm a world-class listener, and I sure would love to help with an issue that doesn't involve my own family for once. It would be a welcome distraction."

She studies my eyes before nodding in acceptance.

"My wife and I have been working through some issues for the last year. I really thought we were getting somewhere, but my friend just called to let me know she saw Erin with another girl tonight. She even took a few pictures from the corner of the bar, in case I didn't believe her."

She slides the cell phone out of her back pocket, and when she swipes it to access the screen, the image is already pulled up. I was hoping there could be a reasonable explanation, but her wife's arm around this stranger in the dark corner booth leaves little room for innocent possibilities. Karli's wife is cheating on her while she's out of town for work. At least my garbage ex-fiancé had the balls to do it while I was in town. All the ridiculous tragedy from the last few months has distracted me from how much I hate the man.

"Karli, I'm sorry. I've been in your position, and it's not easy," I tell her. I'd like to hug her but still feel that I don't know her well enough to invade her personal space, so I lightly place my hand on her arm. "I know it feels like you'll never be okay, but I promise that you will."

"Thank you for not suggesting it could be innocent and that I'm worrying for nothing, like my best friend just did on the phone. I don't need toxic positivity right now; I need the truth."

Much to my surprise, she hugs me. She holds me in the embrace for at least ten seconds, her grip suggesting that she'll break down if she lets go. When she finally does, I grab both of her hands and speak quickly to capture her attention before she loses it again.

"My best advice is to remember that the person who is meant for you wouldn't dream of disrespecting you like this. Your wife should be your best friend, and best friends don't hurt each other like this. You deserve the world and a partner who is your biggest supporter; please don't forget that."

My strategy backfires and Karli begins to sob. By the time she collects herself and thanks me several times for the advice and for listening, the shoulder of my sweatshirt is soaked from her tears. My heart breaks for her. Although my fierce independence didn't allow me to grieve quite this much when Dave cheated on me, I do understand the hurt that comes from such a betrayal.

After Karli is out of sight, I knock lightly on the door of Nolan's cabin; it's a strange feeling to knock on one of our own cabins, but I don't feel comfortable letting myself in quite yet. He swings the door open swiftly, and I'm startled.

"KB, come in. I'm about to get a call from one of my contacts at MSP," he tells me, rapidly motioning for me to come inside, while also frantically pointing to his phone as if he needs to explain how he will be receiving the call. For a journalist from out of town, I'm shocked at how quickly he has made friends with the Michigan State Police. My own sister was missing and I could barely get them to return my calls for years.

"You seem worked up; is it big news?" I ask, kicking my shoes off and taking a seat in the small dining area. He has papers strewn about the table, with his laptop sitting on one of the chairs and small pastel Post-It notes littering nearly every surface of the room.

"I think they found something at Rich's house, Katie," he tells me. He rips a sheet of paper towel off the roll and hands it to me. At first I think it's because he's expecting me to cry but I follow his gaze to my soaked shoulder and realize it's to clean up the mess of tears and mascara Karli left on my shirt.

"*Something*? Like the baby? Did they find the baby?"

He pulls out a chair and sits next to me for all of two

seconds before accepting that he's too wound up and bounces back up to his feet.

"I don't know, but I'm not sure what else they could have found that would qualify as *major news*. The podcast episode where Mal discusses her pregnancy and death of her baby airs tomorrow. If they find her remains today, it's going to be a shitshow for your sister. I am so sorry . . . I would have never dreamed the episode airing could coincide with the discovery of her body," Nolan explains, his bottom lip beginning to quiver as he finishes.

Now, I stand. I take the phone from his hand, set it on the table, and intertwine my fingers with his.

"Nolan, the world is going to find out she was pregnant one way or another. She *chose* for you to be the one to deliver that message. She understands that when the episode airs, it's going to ignite yet another media firestorm. She's ready. She wants to get it over with. If it happens to be the same day they find her baby's remains, that just means we handle it all in one day instead of dealing with it twice. Maybe it's a blessing in disguise."

He appears to consider this before we are interrupted by the buzzing of his phone on the old, wooden table next to us. He nods to me before answering.

"Of course, off the record," he tells whoever is on the other end of the line.

For the next three or four minutes, he paces, nods, and responds with questions like "So, what does that mean?" and "Are you sure?" before ending the call and staring at the floor of the cabin for a beat.

"It's not the baby," he tells me.

"Okay . . . then what is it?" I ask.

"They found a trunk full of video footage buried in Rich's yard. It appears he had a trail cam or two overlooking the bunkers on his land."

"I thought he and Lincoln weren't working together—does this mean he knew what was going on? He knew what Lincoln was doing to those girls?" I don't mean for my tone to be so frantic, but the questions are firing into my mind at an uncontrollable pace.

My hands are shaking. If he has footage of Lincoln bringing girls to the bunker, it's going to answer everyone's questions about timelines and if there are any other victims we don't know about. Since the discovery of his heinous crimes, countless families have come forward, hoping they can get answers about their missing girls, praying Palmer was involved so they can finally have closure. Unfortunately, we all said goodbye to finding answers when Lincoln was killed in prison. These tapes could change everything.

"I don't know what this means about Rich's involvement, but apparently, the tapes are all labeled with descriptions and dates. It also proves he has had accomplices in the past."

The way Nolan looks at me after he says this sends a chill up my spine.

"I'm going to know these accomplices, aren't I?" I ask, not really sure I want to hear the answer.

"They are working on identifying the people in the tapes; the victims and any guilty participants. My source wanted me to know that MSP is going to call in the FBI to help . . . They haven't reviewed all the tapes yet, but they can confirm that several of them are labeled *Nelson*."

"Nelson . . . as in Sheriff Nelson?"

He nods, but I knew the answer before I even asked.

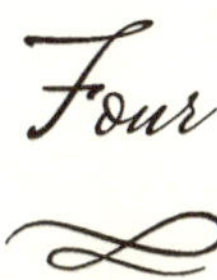

Four

BECAUSE I VALUE my developing relationship with Nolan, I need to keep my word that his confidential sources will remain confidential. He has repeatedly assured me that he will personally notify my family if there's a critical situation they need to know about. Tapes confirming Lincoln Palmer had accomplices, reportedly including the man who was at my birthday breakfast yesterday, don't qualify. I need to keep my mouth shut and let the family find out from the detectives.

Luckily, it doesn't take long. By lunchtime on the day after Nolan received the call from his source at MSP, the lieutenant who showed up at our house days ago arrives at the restaurant. Once again, Lou appears flustered by his presence, and I'm so amused I nearly forget why he's paying a visit to our family business. She speaks with him alone for a moment before asking Dougie to watch the bar so I can step out back and speak with them outside. I throw on my coat as I'm exiting the dining room from the side door to meet them in the gravel parking lot.

I'm no actress, but I do a sufficient job of pretending to be surprised by the news of the tapes. He doesn't mention

Nelson, but he also doesn't include him in the discussion when asking us to come to the station this afternoon to review the footage and see if we can identify anyone. He'd love to have Malorie present for the viewing but understands that she may not feel up to it. I'm not sure she will, considering the footage most likely includes girls being taken against their will to an underground bunker, just like she was. Though they were taken by different men, I imagine there is a great deal of survivor's guilt, knowing that most of those girls will never see their families again.

Lou glances my way to gauge my feelings about including Mal in the process. I shrug. "I'll talk to her after my shift and see if she feels up to it. There aren't any actual assaults on the tapes, correct?"

"The girls appear to be unconscious during the transport. I can skip past those scenes; we are really just looking for your help identifying Palmer's associates. It's a small town, it occurred less than a mile from your home, and it might jog Malorie's memory if she encountered any of these other suspects while in captivity," Lieutenant Barkley tells us.

"Well, if you're just needing help identifying locals, why don't you have Nelson do it? He's lived here as long as I have," Lou offers.

Barkley's silence nearly takes my breath away. He stares down at the gravel in front of his boots and inhales before his eyes travel up to meet hers. I watch Lou's expression, waiting for her to connect the dots. Luckily, it's Lou, so it doesn't take long.

"He's on the fucking tapes, isn't he?" Lou spits out. She begins pacing before Barkley can even answer the question.

"It's an active investigation, ma'am. We would greatly appreciate the cooperation of you and your family." He tips his hat before turning to walk back to his police cruiser.

"Let's call the night crew in early. I think we should talk to

Mal and get over to the station. I can't focus until I know who is on those tapes," Lou tells me once the lieutenant is out of the parking lot. "They better arrest them quick, or I'll strangle every one of them."

"I'm on it," I answer.

I text Nolan and give him a quick rundown of what's happening as I walk back to the lodge after my shift. He responds that he's around whenever I need him and casually mentions that today's release broke a record for his most listened to podcast episode within hours of uploading it. A normal girlfriend would pick up a bottle of champagne and head over to celebrate, but I'm too preoccupied with a kidnapping and murder investigation to do normal girlfriend things. I can't exactly call my life a dumpster fire—I did get my sister back, but the rest has been mildly chaotic. I'm surprised we aren't being hounded by the media yet, but for all I know, Lou's been getting the calls and just ignoring them.

A few small flakes of snow drift down around me, barely visible but enough to remind me that I haven't dug my winter clothes out of storage yet. I usually have that done before my birthday each year, but to say this year has been a little different would be an understatement. I'm usually the friend who responds to texts immediately; yet, I currently have several dozen messages I've left unread for the past few weeks. Everyone wants to know how we are doing, and most of them, understandably, would like to see Mal. I'll get back to them in due time.

Speaking of Mal, she's on the couch when I get upstairs. She's watching an old episode of *Jersey Shore* and turns to me when I walk in.

"Have you seen this? It's on MTV."

I can't help but laugh.

"Yes, Mal, everyone has seen it. God, I've missed you," I

tell her, shaking my head in disbelief again that she's alive and back home.

"Sorry, elitist; some of us spent the last twenty years locked in a basement with three channels."

I walk around the couch and sit next to her. I know she's using humor as a coping mechanism, but it's also just so comforting to joke with her like we did growing up. Complying with Dalia's advice, I try not to ask direct questions about her time in the basement. I let her give me information as she feels comfortable doing so. But since she brought up the subject, I dip my toes in the water with a follow up question.

"Did you have a favorite show to watch down there?" I ask.

She stares past the TV and out the window facing the lake for a few seconds. I hope I didn't mess up by asking her a question. My fears are quelled when I see a slight smile appear.

"My favorite was *Jeopardy* because Rich usually brought dinner down before it started, so I would get to eat while I watched it. He would normally go back upstairs and get drunk, so I wouldn't have to see him again until the next day."

Her answer makes my chest ache. All the years she was gone, whether I was home here at the lodge, working at the restaurant, or in my temporary home of Lansing, I always had *Jeopardy* on. I can't even explain what has drawn me to the show all these years; I always thought of it as my comfort show. Even if I was preoccupied and couldn't give Mr. Trebek my full attention, I would play it in the background. Now I know the sister I yearned for every night was watching the very same show. It's almost too surreal to believe.

"I'd be happy to start making you dinner before *Jeopardy*, but you're out of luck if you think I'm letting you eat alone," I tell her, sinking back into the overstuffed couch cushions and resting my head on her shoulder.

She kisses the top of my head and whispers, "Life is so good."

After all she's been through, those are words I never thought I'd hear her say.

"You did get the memo that Trebek died, right?" I ask.

"What!" she yells, sitting up straight before erupting in a fit of laughter. "Yes, it was a sad day, but Ken Jennings isn't doing half bad."

"No, he sure isn't." I exhale. *And neither are we,* I think.

We are interrupted by Lou arriving upstairs and throwing her apron, keys, and pack of cigarettes in the small wicker basket on the entryway table.

"Well, what's the verdict?" she says, impatience evident in her tone.

"On what?" Mal asks. Her innocent doe eyes kill me. I may be the younger sister, but I'd do anything to protect her from any further harm or stress for as long as she lives. Realistically, I know that's not possible. Irrationally, I'm still going to try.

I sit forward quickly and begin explaining the situation to Mal, getting the words in before Lou can take over because I know my explanation will be much gentler.

"Guys, I'm positive the only man I saw while I was in captivity was Rich. But I'd do anything to catch the bastards who had anything to do with the missing girls, so count me in," she says, nodding with confidence and hopping to her feet. "Let me throw some jeans on and we can go."

"You sure you can handle this, kid?" Lou asks.

"At this point, I don't think there's a damn thing I can't handle, Lou," Mal responds with a wink and a smile before disappearing down the hall.

Once we hear the bedroom door shut, Lou makes a noise so loud I physically jump in response. For a minute, I think she's choking on something. I jump to my feet and spin around to find her eyes red, with tears streaming down her face. This is not Brenda or Deb; this is Lou . . . who never cries.

"Lou! What happened?" I gasp and run to her side.

"Ah, Christ, kid. I think it just hit me is all. You and Mal are both back home and I think she's gonna be alright. That's all I've wanted in this life for the last twenty years and now I've got it. I can die a happy woman."

"Well, we still need your ass here to run the show, so don't go dying on us anytime soon," I say, giving her shoulders a squeeze. I know a full-on hug isn't something Lou Benard welcomes, even in life's most emotional moments.

She wipes her eyes with a scratchy paper towel, despite there being a full box of soft tissues on the end table just feet from her. The woman never cries, so I cut her some slack.

A few moments later, I hear the unmistakable sound of Dougie's dumbass whistling as he ascends the back stairs to the family lodge. He must be feeling better. I recognize the song as Nat King Cole's "Almost Like Being in Love," and I reluctantly smile because it was in one of the *Grumpy Old Men* movies, which Mal, Dougie, and I watched on repeat growing up. The song reminds me of simpler, happier times.

Mal exits our room just as Dougie arrives in the lodge and singsongs, "Well if it isn't three of the most beautiful women I've ever seen." The three of us shoot panicked looks to each other, wondering if the body snatchers have arrived in Grady, Michigan, because this can't be our Dougie.

"Do you need money or something, kid?" Lou barks.

Dougie laughs entirely too loud.

"You're not on that funny stuff, are you? The wacky tobacky?" she asks, leaning forward to inspect his pupils.

"Lou, you kill me. I'm just in a good mood. It's almost Thanksgiving—your favorite holiday. You should be just as happy." He squeezes her shoulder before kicking off his shoes and heading down the hall to his bedroom.

"The three of us are going to run some errands," I yell in his direction and catch the attention of both Lou and Mal, who know it's best not to let him come with us to the station.

"You girls have fun," he yells back. "I'm hopping in the shower and then going to hang out with Chelsey for the night. Don't wait up." He spins to give us an exaggerated wink before disappearing into his room.

Five

WE ARE OVER AN HOUR DEEP, and on our fourth tape of footage from the bunkers, when Lou asks for a smoke break. So far, we've seen Lincoln bringing several girls to the bunker—which Barkley thankfully fast-forwarded through but will be comparing to the photos of missing girls from the Midwest—Sheriff Nelson hunting on the property and stepping over the bunker doors like he didn't know they were there, and Rich adjusting and/or cleaning the cameras countless times. When Lincoln would visit the bunkers, it sent a chill down my spine to see him arrive with gallon jugs of water and loaves of bread. If the girls were lucky, he'd also bring a jar of peanut butter. Lou's fists had clenched and tightened several times, which convinced me that if Lincoln wasn't already dead, she'd find a way to get in that jail and kill him herself.

While Lou steps out the back door with lighter in hand, Barkley escorts Mal and me to the bathroom, and I realize the last time I was at this police station long enough to need a restroom break, I was being questioned after her disappearance. Mom, Dougie, the aunts, and I were put in separate

28

rooms and forced to account for our whereabouts, as well as anything we could remember about the last time we saw her. We were asked if she could have run away, could have met someone online, could have been secretly depressed enough to end her own life. The out-of-town detectives suggested every possible outcome and most of them blamed Malorie for being gone. I hope they all felt horrible when the news broke that she was being held underground by a monster while they insisted she'd turn back up on her own with an apology for leaving us. *You ladies need to accept that some girls just don't want to be found. She's technically an adult, and disappearing isn't a crime.*

When the toilet flushes and Mal comes out of the stall to wash her hands, I pull her into an embrace. After stiffening slightly, she relaxes and hugs me back.

"Let me guess, just happy to have me home?" she asks.

"You're catching on," I whisper in her ear.

Lou and Barkley are back in the small, windowless room when we reenter. She's chewing on a mint to disguise her breath, and if I'm not mistaken, she also gave herself a few squirts from the White Diamonds perfume bottle in the glovebox. Mal reads my mind and raises her eyebrows a few times in my direction.

"So, all the tapes with Nelson's name on them seem to just be of the man hunting or bringing bait to his pile. Is there a chance he's not actually involved in this?" Lou asks, and I know she's mentally willing that to be the truth. I'm not sure she could handle another man she thought she knew turning out to be a monster.

"We've got a few tapes left, but you're right that we don't have any damning evidence yet. Once we finish reviewing all the footage and conclude the investigation, confirming his non-involvement, Nelson will be brought back from administrative leave," Barkley tells her.

"With an apology, I hope," Mal adds.

"He most certainly will get my sincerest apology, but I also know Nelson would be taking the same steps if it were my name on those tapes. I assure you, he understands the process."

Barkley leans forward and plugs the next USB into his computer. The scene that pops up when he clicks on the file is an empty shot of the bunkers, but I can tell the footage is from years ago, based on the height and fullness of the trees. They've reduced dramatically in size from the tapes we had been reviewing, and the quality of the video is grainier than the previous ones, which suggests it was an older model camera.

Confirming our suspicions, a much younger Lincoln Palmer comes into view. I steal a glance at Malorie, remembering that this was the man she believed she was in love with twenty years ago. On appearance alone, I get the appeal. He was fit, tan, and his chiseled jaw looked like something from the cover of a romance novel. If that baby had survived, there's no doubt she would have been stunning. Sure, we'd have to worry that she inherited her father's sociopathic tendencies, but she'd certainly be a looker.

Lincoln is motioning to someone off camera and we all hold our breath as he comes into view, carrying an unconscious girl over his shoulder like a sack of potatoes. Something about his gait, even while carrying the girl, is so familiar to me. A quick glance at Mal and Lou tells me they feel the same. I can't quite place it, but I know this man.

My heart stops when he sets the girl down on the ground and opens the bunker door while Lincoln watches. The man takes survey of his surroundings, even glancing up in the trees and appearing to look directly at the camera. Barkley pauses the video and zooms in on his face. The three of us gasp in unison, with Mal placing a shaking hand over her heart and whispering, "No . . ." before a single tear rolls down her cheek.

"Ladies, I know this is hard to watch, and we all knew the possibility that at least one of the men on this video would be someone you have intimate knowledge of, given the size of this town. Is this . . . your father?" Barkley asks.

Now I'm crying, too, and Lou is leaning forward, head in her hands. I shake my head but can't find the strength to say the words out loud. It's not our father on the tape, but it's a man we've known our entire lives.

"No, it's Dougie's. That man is Brenda's ex-husband, and his name is Dennis Coleman. You better hope you find him before I do, Lieutenant Barkley."

IN SEVERAL OF THE VIDEOS, Dennis doesn't go down into the bunkers. He paces back and forth, dragging his boots through the fallen leaves scattered around the bunker doors, flicking the lid of his lighter open and closed. I can't be certain, but I think it's the same lighter that Dad and Sheriff Nelson had for years until I watched them get thrown away at my birthday party a few days ago. My Uncle Dennis stood as a groomsman beside my dad and Sheriff Nelson at Rich's wedding to Nicole's mother, where they all received lighters and flasks as their groomsmen gifts. We have an entire photo album in the basement of the nuptials, featuring half the town of Grady laughing, drinking, and dancing into the early hours of the night. Who would have guessed that at least two members of that wedding party would become violent predators and tarnish the good name of Grady?

After Dennis' last appearance on the tapes, Barkley pauses our little viewing party and calls for another visiting detective to join us. I look around the room, and it's no surprise to see that Mal and Lou look as exhausted as I feel. We thought we were done with surprises, only to find that a man we considered family for decades played an active role in the most shocking crimes this area has ever seen. For the past twenty minutes, the three of us have been staring blankly at the footage, barely reacting each time Dennis came into frame. Lincoln Palmer, Rich Lowery, and now Dennis Coleman were all men we *thought* we knew. It will make us question every man's intentions for the rest of our lives, I'm sorry to admit. It's one thing to find out a man you know did something disappointing; it's an entirely different game when those men live next door and you find out they are monsters who have walked among us, their crimes undetected for years.

I haven't seen Dennis since the summer after my freshman year of college, when I came home because I couldn't afford a summer apartment off campus. The aunts were never fans of his because, among countless other faults, he put *everything* above the needs of his family. Any free time he had was spent gambling—on slots, on cards, on football, on anything you could make a wager, really. He couldn't hold down a job for longer than six months at a time and always seemed to conveniently forget when Dougie had a school play or baseball game. Although my own father came around later in life, I knew what it was like to be the kid without a father at your events. It sucked. At least Dougie, Mal, and I had each other. We also had our mothers, our aunts, and the support of half of this sleepy town at most of our games, school plays, and competitions. Having a father present would have been nice, but we had more than enough love coming from thirty different directions when we needed it the most.

Within ten minutes, the detective Barkley called arrives and introduces himself as Owen. I'm not sure if that's his first or his last name, but I'm also realistic about my chances of remembering half of these out-of-town officers and detectives, so I just nod politely as we take turns introducing ourselves. He's handsome in a classic way, with dark skin and hair and a slim but muscular build. He sits in a chair next to Barkley and pulls out an old, ratty notebook. It makes me laugh because I haven't been questioned by a detective in years, but I thought surely by now they'd be using iPads or some form of similar technology for their interview notes.

"When is the last time any of you saw Dennis Coleman?"

Lou and I look at each other, trying to remember how long it's been since a family member has mentioned encountering the asshole, while leaving Malorie out of the conversation because she's been underground for twenty years and won't be contributing anything to the conversation.

"The last memory I have of seeing him is on Memorial Day weekend after my freshman year of college. He got drunk at the parade in downtown Grady and Brenda left crying. They got in a huge blowout, and he left. I figured he'd be back after a day or two, like he always was, but he didn't come back that summer. It was no loss, I assure you," I tell him with zero concern for my lack of empathy. He can't arrest me for thinking the man is useless.

"And you?" he asks Lou. She blows out a puff of air so fierce her bangs break free of their Aqua Net hold and flutter slightly.

"Not that I'd like to think of that son of a bitch any longer than I need to, but he came back that fall for a few weeks. Didn't last long; it was the same shit every time he tried to come back home and pretend to be a good man so he could finesse Brenda for a place to stay and a few hot meals. He took cash from Brenda's nightstand and went to the casino in Manistique. When she found out, she told him he was out for good. Against all of our expectations, she's kept her word. We haven't seen him since."

Barkley chimes in.

"Has anyone heard from him at all? Phone calls? Texts? Any last known locations?"

"Yeah, he texts Dougie every year on his birthday. Never a phone call or a visit, just a fucking text because that's what men like him do. It's all they're capable of. It's typically from a different phone number each year, and I'm assuming that's because he can't handle paying a phone bill long enough to have anything but a prepaid."

"And does he mention to Dougie where he's staying when he sends these texts?" Owen asks.

"Not that I'm aware of, but we can ask Dougie when he gets home. He's out with his little girlfriend tonight."

"We'd love to get him down here and ask him a few questions about his father. Would you like to be the one to tell him about the tapes? Sometimes this news is easier coming from family," Barkley suggests.

"Yeah, it shouldn't be too hard of a pill to swallow. He already knows his father is useless. Now we can add kidnapping and assault to the list of reasons why," Lou answers dryly. "I have just as much interest as you in seeing Dennis caught, and I'll do whatever I can to make that happen," she adds.

This seems to appease both Barkley and Owen, as they nod to each other and Owen excuses himself from the small room, which already felt cramped with the four of us before he arrived.

"Alright, ladies. We just have two tapes left, and I'm anxious to have you view them because they contain the last two unidentified suspects. We're almost done here."

"What's a few more minutes when we can add two more men to the list of Grady's finest assholes?" I say, relaxing back into my chair for our next feature film.

"Well, these two suspects aren't Grady's finest men. They are both women," Barkley answers.

This causes all three of us to sit up straighter in our chairs. *Women?*

"You're telling me that women were involved in the

kidnapping of these girls? How could females be responsible for this?" Malorie asks him. She hesitates before asking, "Is . . . is Mae Lowery on the tapes? Was she helping Lincoln?"

She's keeping her composure, but her knee has begun bouncing, and she's tapping one finger at a time on the side of her jeans.

"I'm sorry, I'm not familiar with Mae Lowery. I'm assuming that was Rich's mother? I'll play the tapes quickly for you; I understand how difficult it will be if someone else you know is shown on this footage."

He leans forward, plugs a USB into the county-owned laptop and presses play.

"I'm going to show you the older video first. We believe this was taken shortly after the bunkers were constructed."

Once again, Lincoln comes into frame first. This time, the girl with him is conscious and walking, but barely. She is either hammered drunk or has been drugged; I'm assuming the latter. Lincoln is holding her up by her elbow, but not kindly. He is jerking her with each step and seems frustrated that he's having to help at all. He stops at the entrance to the bunker and shouts something to someone standing off camera. These trail cams don't have sound, but I can safely assume whatever he's yelling isn't pleasant. A few seconds later, a woman comes into view with a pile of blankets and a pillow. Much like Dennis Coleman in the earlier videos, she looks around nervously. It only takes seconds for me to recognize her as Lincoln's ex-wife, JoAnne Palmer.

"She knew," I say, barely louder than a whisper. "She knew he was a monster."

"You know this woman?" Barkley asks.

"That's JoAnne. She's Lincoln Palmer's ex-wife. The issue is, by the time they moved to Grady Lake, they were already divorced, and he was married to Fallon. So why in the world would any woman, let alone his ex-wife, be helping him with these crimes?" Lou asks.

"She told me at Benson's funeral that Lincoln might have something to do with Sammie Spencer's disappearance. When I asked her about it again last week while she and Bradford were pulling out of town in their U-Haul, she denied ever saying it to me. She told me I must have misunderstood her."

Lou shoots me a look that confirms she's going to have my ass later for not telling her about my conversations with JoAnne. Everything happened so fast, I haven't had the chance to tell Lou a lot of things.

"Sounds to me like she had a change of heart and regrets her earlier actions, so she tried to give you a heads up so you'd save Sammie. She probably considered it redemption for her earlier sins. Unfortunately for JoAnne, accessory to murder doesn't have a statute of limitations, so she's going to have a lot more redeeming to do," Barkley says.

"You said there's one more unidentified woman helping Palmer on these tapes. Can we watch it so we can get out of here?" Malorie asks.

Barkley nods and rifles through his evidence bags to retrieve the final USB.

"You good?" I ask Mal.

"Yeah, I just have a bit of a headache. I think I want to go back to the lodge and lie down."

"We'll make it quick; I'll fast forward to the part where you can see the suspect's face," Barkley tells us all, but his eyes are focused on Malorie.

When the clip begins, I can tell the footage is recent by the surroundings and the quality of the camera. It's crystal clear. We all gasp when we see a conscious but clearly medicated Sammie Spencer stumbling to the bunker, with a woman about the same size as her holding her up by the elbow. She has a maroon ski mask on, which sends chills down my spine.

Long blonde strands of hair are exposed, trailing down her back beneath the mask. I begin mentally flipping through every blonde I know in this county.

She leads Sammie underground, and they both remain there for a few seconds before Barkley leans forward to skip through the footage. I can see the timestamp on the bottom of the screen; it's nearly five minutes before he stops the tape and the woman reappears above ground, this time alone. She's about to lock the trap door when something captures her attention off camera. She turns her head, pulls her ski mask off, and smiles when Lincoln Palmer comes into view. The young woman stands straight and wraps her arm around his neck, kissing him passionately on the lips. Once they part, she looks in the direction of the trail cam and smiles, just like she did to me when she was kissing my cousin at The Moose Trap.

The woman in the video is Benard's Lakeside Inn's newest employee, Chelsey. The same woman who is currently alone with our cousin, Dougie.

Seven

"WHAT HAVE YOU GOT?" Lou barks from behind the steering wheel as she flies through town toward the resort.

"Nobody at the restaurant has seen him, Brenda wants to know why we are looking for him, and Nicole hasn't read my text yet," I respond, my eyes closed and right hand gripping the oh-shit handle. I get violently ill riding passenger on a normal day. Feeling tired, hungry, and panicked while Lou drives like she's an extra in *Mad Max* is throttling my nausea into overdrive. I'd ask her to pull over so I can throw up, but we only have one mile left and nobody bothers Lou when she's in panic mode.

"Nic's at the Grab N Go, call the store," she instructs.

She answers on the second ring.

"What do you want, you little bitch?"

Glad to see the store's caller ID is still working, considering the phone is at least old enough to vote.

"Have you seen Dougie today?"

"Yeah, his dumbass just stopped in to buy wine, and he didn't get it in a box so this date must be serious."

"Nic, where was he going? Tell me everything he said."

"Damn, KB, since when do you give a shit what Douglas is doing? Wait . . . are we pranking him? We going to fuck up his room? I can be there in fifteen."

I slap my hand on the center console in frustration, just as Lou pulls into the gravel parking lot behind the lodge. "Nic, listen to me. I don't have time to explain. Where was he going?"

"Katie, I don't know. He mentioned the swans, but I reminded him it's too early in the season to see them. I had other customers, so he paid and left. What's going on?"

"I'll call you back," I tell her, ending the call. "Apparently, he mentioned John's Lake to Nicole, but she told him the swans weren't there yet. That's all she's got," I tell Lou and Mal.

We all hurriedly exit the car while Lou barks out directions to us.

"Mal, check the lodge and keep trying to call his cell from Deb's; she always leaves it next to the coffee maker when she goes to work. The passcode is 1-2-3-4 because she's a dumbass. Keep it on you so we can get ahold of you when we find him. I'll run over to the restaurant to make sure nobody has talked to him. Katie, take a quick drive out to John's Lake and make sure he didn't take her there anyway."

We all nod, and I reach in my bag for the keys to my Highlander, which is parked a few yards away from Lou's vehicle. "We don't actually think she'd hurt Dougie, do we?"

"You saw her on the tape, Katie," Malorie answers. My stomach turns. She's absolutely right. I may give Dougie a hard time, but I love him like a brother. We can't lose him.

"Go," Lou yells as she jogs toward the back of the restaurant, the closest thing to exercise I've seen her perform in decades.

I rarely speed, but I know any officer in this town will let me off the hook the minute I explain where I'm going. Nearly all the tourists have gone home for the off-season, so I'm not worried about drivers who don't know the backroads. When I get to the turn off for John's Lake Road, my heart flutters remembering the last time I was here, with Nolan. I was worried about Mal, and we sat in my car by the lake as I poured my heart out to him. That might have been the first time I thought seriously about a future with the man who had been a stranger just weeks before. Now that we're officially a couple—well, at least I think we are—I wonder what our lives will be like when the dust settles and there isn't constant chaos surrounding us. The idea of a lazy Sunday morning with him, reading the newspaper and going for a stroll around the lake, is almost too foreign to consider a real possibility. Are we just clinging to each other because we have the shared trauma of everything that's happened in the past few weeks? Only time will tell.

My heartbeat intensifies when I see a small sedan parked on the edge of the lake. I'm not sure what Chelsey drives, but somehow, I picture her vehicle looking just like this. I throw my SUV into park behind the car, blocking it in so she can't leave. I fly out so quickly I leave my driver's side door hanging wide open.

I run around to the front of the car and slap my hand on the hood while looking through the windshield. Staring back at me are two wide-eyed teenagers, faces red and flushed. *Shit.*

"My bad, carry on! Only do things you're comfortable doing; don't let him pressure you!" I yell as I race back to my car. Not my finest moment, but you know what they say about desperate times.

Stomping my foot on the gas pedal, I navigate the gravel road around the lake like it's a backwoods racetrack, kicking dust up behind me as I go. There are no more cars parked at the lake. I reach over and grab my cell to call Deb's phone, which Malorie hopefully has with her by now. It takes a few minutes for me to come back into range and I hit dial as soon as a bar of service shows up on my screen.

"Find him?" she answers, panic evident in her voice.

"No," I tell her, not bothering to ask the same question because obviously she hasn't seen him either.

"Lou?" I ask.

"Haven't seen her since we got here, but her car is gone now. She must be out chasing leads."

I don't answer immediately because I'm thinking. I'm wracking my brain for anywhere they would have gone on a date if they wanted privacy.

"Check his Insta," I tell Mal.

"What does that mean?" she asks in earnest. *Fuck*. I pull the car off on the side of the road.

"Hold on, I'll do it," I say. I pull up the Instagram app and search for Dougie, whose screenname is some foolish, misspelled reference to one of his favorite video games. He hasn't posted in over a month, but I can tell by the circle around his profile picture that he's posted something to his stories. I click on it with shaking hands.

He has three stories posted. The first is a screenshot of the dinner special at Benard's tonight. *Great job, Dougie. I'm sure your twenty-seven followers will give us a real sales boost.* The second is a picture of the wine he bought at Nicole's store with a heart emoji. He went all out and bought a bottle of *Josh* brand wine that costs nearly twenty dollars from the Grab N Go, which is about fifteen dollars higher than his normal budget. I inhale so sharply I nearly choke when I view his third story. It's a picture of our lake, but it's from the opposite side, from Palmer's Resort. The font over the picture says, "The whole resort to ourselves."

"He's at Palmer's," I quickly say to Mal, who has remained on the line while I scrolled through Instagram. "He's at the abandoned resort."

"Head that way now. I'll call Lou to meet you there," she says before hanging up.

I switch on my hazard lights and floor it. I sincerely hope I encounter one of Grady's finest on my drive because I'm going to need backup anyway. We gave Barkley the names of JoAnne and Chelsey nearly an hour ago now, but I'm not sure how long it takes to get arrest warrants ready. These aren't things I've had to concern myself with before the events of this crazy year.

It takes me less than ten minutes to fly past the tacky, ornate Palmer's Resort sign off the main road. I take a sharp right; I'm not sure exactly what building I'm looking for, but this is the angle Dougie took the picture from. Sure enough, I see one of the Benard's rental pontoon boats tied to the end of the dock at the resort as I pull into a parking spot. The minute I slam my door shut, I hear Lou's car flying down the drive. I'm not sure where she was when Mal called her, but she obviously drove here like a bat out of hell.

"The picture was posted from here!" I yell as she exits her car and runs in my direction.

"Douglas!" she shouts as we jog toward the waterfront, both of us darting our eyes in every possible direction, looking for movement. "Doug Benard!"

Off to our right, we see someone exit one of the small employee cabins and sprint to the docked Benard's boat. She has her hair tucked under a baseball cap, but I'm certain it's Chelsey. She runs down the dock and leaps into the waiting boat, reaching forward to untie the knot and throw the rope back onto the deck of the boat.

"Chelsey, wait! Where is Dougie?" I yell, my tennis shoes sinking into the sandy beach as I make my way to her. Her cold, blue eyes stare a hole right through me as she silently puts the boat in reverse and maneuvers around before flooring it away from us, ignoring the no-wake buoys.

"Katie!" Lou screams, and I spin to see her in the doorway of the small cabin Chelsey just exited. Before I can even register what's happening enough to turn and run to her, she has disappeared inside.

I sprint, once again slowed by the soft sand of the beach, and gain momentum once I'm on the grass. Nearly out of breath, I reach the cabin and grab the door frame to steady myself.

In the small, scarcely decorated log cabin I find Lou on the ground, performing CPR on the lifeless body of my cousin, Dougie.

Eight

THE DÉJÀ VU from standing in the private family waiting room of the hospital is unreal. Somehow making it even stranger is the fact that Malorie is in the waiting room with us now, alive and well.

Pacing back and forth over the tightly woven gray carpet next to the world's most uncomfortable vinyl armchairs is so depressing it's nearly comical. I'd have a good, hard laugh if it weren't for being sick with worry, not knowing if Dougie is going to come out of this alive. Our lives have all been marked by one singular tragedy before this year—the disappearance of my sister. For twenty years, we struggled, we fought, we cried, but Malorie being gone *was* our tragedy. It defined our family and was most certainly the primary topic of conversation whenever the Benard name was mentioned anywhere in this state. Now it seems we can't catch a break. They say these things happen in threes, but I've lost count of how many hits we've taken since I arrived home from Lansing.

I shake my head in disbelief when the doctor comes in to give us an update. It's the same doctor who came to inform us of Malorie's condition after her rescue. The realization in his eyes that he's once again dealing with the Benard family is quickly replaced by compassion, which tells me he isn't here to give us good news.

"The family of Douglas Benard?" he asks to confirm, although he knows damn well who we are. He makes eye contact with Malorie and flinches slightly at her presence. "Miss Benard, it's very nice to see you. I wish it were under better circumstances. I am very sorry to learn of your loss, but happy to see you looking so well."

Sorry for her loss? *Ah, the podcast episode. He knows about the death of her baby.*

Malorie gives a tight smile and nods in response. We all just want to hear how Dougie is doing. Brenda looks worse than she did at my mom's funeral, which was the worst I had ever seen her look. I'm not sure how we are going to break the news about her ex-husband, but that's a problem for tomorrow.

"There are two separate issues we're tackling here. Douglas suffered some pretty severe trauma to the back of his head, most likely one hard blow by a singular object, based on the injury. He also has ingested a near-fatal dose of the drug fentanyl. We've already administered Naloxone, which can rapidly reverse the effects of an overdose. The trauma to his head is our main concern at the moment. We won't know the extent of the damage until he wakes up."

"And when will that be? When will my baby wake up?" Brenda asks, her hands shaking so violently that she drops the used tissue she'd been clutching for the better part of an hour.

"There's no way to tell for sure, but we are optimistic that it won't be long, Miss Benard. I assure you we are doing everything we can to take great care of your son," the doctor tells her.

"You know he's not a drug user, right? That girl drugged

him. She tried to kill him," Brenda shouts. Deb rushes to her side and wraps her arms around Brenda.

"It wouldn't matter if he was," the doctor assures her. "I promise you we'd be treating him with the same care."

Doctors never seem to hug the shoulders or squeeze the hands of those they are delivering bad news to. I wonder if this is something they are taught in medical school so they don't get emotionally attached to the patient's families, or if it's just a result of having to give news like this every time they arrive for a shift at the hospital. Maybe in the first few years after residency, he did show emotion. Maybe that part of him has died.

"If one or two of you would like to come sit by his bed until he wakes up, that would be fine. Just check in at the station at the end of the hallway," he tells us, taking a few steps back toward the door. His eyes scan the room, briefly landing on each one of us before adding, "I'm sincerely sorry your family is in this waiting room again. Lord knows you've been through enough."

"Who is coming with me?" Brenda asks as soon as the doctor is out of sight.

"Not Deb; he doesn't need to see *two* emotional broads when he wakes up," Lou answers.

Brenda and Deb both tut at the same time, which makes the rest of us smile.

"I'll go," Malorie says. "It's about time I get to be here for someone else."

Nobody argues. Brenda reaches back and grabs Mal's skinny hand before they disappear down the hallway. Deb, Lou, and I collapse into the stupid vinyl torture chairs out of pure exhaustion. Nobody speaks because what is there to say? We got word about thirty minutes ago that Sheriff Nelson was officially cleared of any wrongdoing, and the entire department is currently on the hunt for Chelsey. Our family's rental boat was found abandoned near the north cove. The same cove that Sammie Spencer's body was found in last week and close to where Benson Palmer died. There are only two roads out of Grady, and both have been blocked by officers. This is a great plan, assuming Chelsey hasn't already skipped town.

"Dennis was on the tapes, Deb," Lou says so quietly and calmly you'd swear she was telling her what she's got cooking in the crockpot for dinner tonight.

Deb turns to her with wide eyes.

"With . . . with the girls?" she asks.

Lou nods. Deb's eyes dart over to me, and I nod as well.

"Who else knows?"

"Malorie and the detectives. We need to talk to Dougie to see if Dennis has said anything about where he's living," I respond, a lump in my throat forming when I realize that the casual plan of *talking to Dougie* isn't a guarantee. Not until he wakes up.

"Who is going to tell Brenda?" Deb asks.

"I will. Let's just figure out what's going on with Dougie first. Deal?" Lou offers.

"Deal," Deb quietly responds.

The door to the waiting room bangs open like a shotgun and each of us nearly jump out of our chairs. It's Dad and Nicole. I'm not sure who called them or if they drove together, but they are both here. They search our eyes for any indication of Dougie's condition.

"They are waiting for him to wake up. It appears he ingested fentanyl and was hit pretty hard in the back of the head. We found him unconscious in Chelsey's cabin," Lou explains.

"I think every officer in a three-county radius is out looking for her, judging by all the cars we saw on the drive over," Dad tells us. "We'll get her, and she'll pay. Any idea why she'd do this to Doug?"

"She was on the tapes," I say. "She was working with

Palmer." I barely get the words out before Nolan arrives in the room, much quieter than Dad and Nicole's entrance but with just as much urgency in his pace.

"Chelsey was working with Palmer?" Nolan says, his face reddening slightly when the entire room turns to look at him. "Also, I just ran into Mal in the hallway, and she gave me the rundown on Dougie. I'm so sorry." He lowers his eyes, clasps his hands together under his chin, and performs a quick bowing motion. Heaven help me, I adore this awkward man. "Are you sure it's her on the footage?"

"Nolan, it was her. She was Palmer's accomplice when Sammie was taken. We saw her leading Sammie to the bunker," I tell him.

"That's not possible. She was our server at Benard's the night before we were supposed to do the interview. Sammie barely acknowledged her," he counters.

"Chelsey is wearing a ski mask in the tapes, but you said Sammie was acting a little strange during dinner. Maybe something about Chelsey's voice or mannerisms jogged her memory," I offer.

"So what was her motive for hurting Douglas?" Dad asks.

"We don't know. Maybe he started sniffing around and figured out what she was up to?" Deb suggests.

"We're talking about Dougie here," Lou quips. "He ain't exactly Columbo."

"Maybe he saw something he wasn't supposed to, so she tried to take him out," Nicole suggests.

We all consider the option, which seems the most likely. We've established that Chelsey is a psychopath, but something must have happened for her to take her anger out on Doug. She must have seen him as some sort of threat. Unfortunately, we won't be getting any answers until Dougie wakes up and starts talking.

Nine

NICOLE and I ride back to the resort with Nolan; me in the driver's seat, Nolan beside me and Nicole and Karli in the back. Every man I've dated has given me shit about wanting to drive due to my motion sickness, yet Nolan tossed me the keys without protest. Another check in the "pros" column for Mr. Out-of-Town Podcaster.

He stays quiet for most of the drive, gazing out the window at the endless forest. The trees that were lush and vibrant just weeks ago are now nearly bare and surrounded by dead, fallen leaves. There's a strange feeling in the air when winter is about to creep in and take hold, one I'll never be able to explain to outsiders. Everything is still, like the entire town is holding its breath and waiting for mother nature to let them know she's on her way, and she's not coming quietly. Winters around here are not for the weak of heart.

I'm exhausted enough to ignore Nicole unabashedly shooting her shot in the back seat. Luckily, Karli seems okay with it, so I feel better about letting it happen. Nic's signature move is to discover one fact about the girl she's trying to woo and then ask countless follow up questions, so the unsuspecting target feels showered with attention. It always amuses me because she can't manage to remember a damn thing I say after three decades of friendship, yet she's currently all ears back there listening to Karli describe every detail of her serving job at a diner, back when she was a teenager.

"I bet you were everyone's favorite. Was there like a line of old men waiting to sit in your section every day? You were probably employee of the month."

"Oh my gosh, I actually was employee of the month!" Karli exclaims.

"No way," Nicole replies, leaning over to touch Karli's knee as she says it. I roll my eyes in the rearview mirror, wishing Nic would see me. Stealing a glance at Nolan, I see that he shares my feelings of the obnoxious flirtation.

After a few more seconds of considering the situation, I decide to bite my tongue. Nicole just survived the worst month of her life, and Karli recently learned her wife was cheating. If they want to have a little harmless back-and-forth to make themselves feel better, so be it.

By the time we pull back into Benard's, Nicole and Karli have made plans to walk over to the Grab N Go so Nic can show her the new flavor of Skittles, which may even be a sexual reference I'm not hip enough to be privy to. I need to go up to the lodge and pack Deb and Brenda an overnight bag so they can stay at the hospital with Dougie. Lou said if I pack a duffle bag and leave it by the door, she'll pick it up later when she brings Mal back, and then she'll bring the bag to them at the hospital after the dinner shift. She, of course, is coming back to town to work the dinner shift because heaven forbid she let me handle it.

"It's your night off, kid. Go spend it doing something fun," she'd told me before we left.

I'm not sure how much fun I can have while I worry about Dougie being unconscious and suffering from possible brain damage, but I'll take a free night with Nolan when I can get it. I have no idea when he plans to head back to Chicago, so I'm going to do my best to enjoy the time we have.

"Do you have work to do?" I ask him after I finish packing supplies for Brenda and Deb. Comfortable clothes to sleep in, toothbrushes, night cream, and a few romance novels are snuggly zipped into a duffle bag with a Tito's Vodka logo on the side. The aunts like to leverage our strong seasonal sales with their local liquor reps to get free branded merchandise. They don't care if it's an item we would ever need or use; they take pride in knowing they got it for free. When they are bragging about how they *got one over* on the reps, I never have the heart to tell them that the reps don't pay for the swag, either. I let them have their moments of glory.

"I have a little editing to do before Monday's episode is ready for release, but it doesn't have to be done tonight," Nolan tells me. "Why don't you give me thirty minutes to go shower, and then you can come to the cabin and we'll figure out something to do for dinner?"

"That sounds perfect," I say. It almost feels like a normal date night.

I rush to the bathroom for a quick shower the minute he's out the door. Although there isn't a restaurant in this county with a dress code, I do pick one of my nicer blouses to throw on over jeans for dinner. I recently read an article about how putting effort into how you look when you leave the house creates a plethora of psychological benefits, so I decided to give it a whirl. Knocking the dust off my makeup might also have something to do with trying to impress Nolan, but it also can't hurt to put a little more effort into my appearance. I had a real wake-up call a few weeks ago when I did a load of my laundry and realized it was entirely comprised of work uniforms, pajamas, and sweatpants. If I buy anymore cozy socks, my drawer won't be able to close.

I check the outside temperature on my phone before deciding that my wool peacoat is necessary for the chilly evening air and lock the door behind me while I'm still pulling on my ankle boots. After I jog down a few steps, I see someone standing outside the back door of the lodge. At first, I think it's Nolan, so I begin to smile at the thought of him "picking me up" for our date, despite his cabin being located mere yards away. After he turns slightly, I recognize the chiseled jaw of Bradford Palmer. My stomach drops when I remember his mom's appearance on the tapes. Should I have called to tell him? No, that was in no way my responsibility. It is absolutely devastating that he lost his brother and then learned both of his parents were monsters, but it wasn't my job to deliver the news.

"Katie," he says as I open the door. I recognize the pale skin and bloodshot eyes as the same symptoms of sleep-deprived devastation my family has experienced entirely too often lately. "They arrested my mom. They said she had some-thing to do with everything that went down with my dad."

I flinch a little when he refers to the kidnappings, assault, and murder of several girls as "everything that went down with my dad," but I cut him a break. I'm not sure how I'd describe it if we were talking about my father, either.

"What did they tell you?" I ask him.

"Nothing. They won't tell me anything. She told me to call her lawyer as they were putting her in the police car, so I did, but he won't tell me anything either."

"I'm so sorry, Bradford. I'm not sure I can help you. You might go down to the station and see if Nelson will talk to you," I suggest.

"When we stopped here on our way out of town, you said my mom told you that Dad had something to do with Sammie Spencer. I know she denied it, but I also know you wouldn't make something like that up. Did she know about Sammie

Spencer because she helped? I didn't even know my parents still spoke, let alone went on fucking crime sprees together."

I want to tell him so badly that she only appeared on the tapes from decades ago. Yes, she was guilty of assisting him, but it appeared she came to her senses and stopped. She wasn't on any of the recent footage. She had been replaced by Chelsey. She only had the hunch about Lincoln's involvement with Sammie's disappearance because she knew he was capable of it; she saw it firsthand years ago.

"Bradford, I really think you need to go talk to Nelson. I'm sure he can answer all these questions. I'm so sorry for everything you've gone through this year, I sincerely am."

I reach forward to give his arm a comforting squeeze, but he loses his composure before I can make contact.

"Do you know what it feels like to be all alone, Katie? No, you don't. You have an entire family. Everyone I love is dead or in jail, and you won't even tell me what you fucking know about my mom's arrest? Fuck you, Katie. Fuck. You."

Spit is flying from his mouth as he continues to go off on me. I allow it to happen because I don't think he'd ever physically harm me; he just needs a verbal punching bag as an escape for all the anger he has bottled up, and I'm fine with it being me. I nod as he continues to launch into his tirade about how unfair life is. He's right. It's entirely unfair.

"Hey, that's about enough," Nolan yells, running up the path from his rented cabin. "Back up."

Bradford holds both of his palms up in defeat, taking two slow steps backward. Tears are now streaming down his face. This poor, poor man looks exactly like the boy I met all those years ago when his family arrived in Grady. I see it in his eyes—he's lost.

Against my better judgement, I leap forward and hug him. I place my right hand on the back of his head and gently guide it to my shoulder. For minutes, he simply cries. Nolan stays at a safe distance but close enough to intervene if need be.

"I'm sorry, KB," Bradford chokes out.

"There's nothing to be sorry about. I know you're hurt, and it's a different kind of hurt than I've experienced, you're right. Everything's going to be okay, even if you don't think it's possible right now," I assure him. I pull back out of our embrace and pull a small pack of tissues out of my bag, handing them over.

His face flushes when he looks at Nolan and apologizes to him, as well.

"It's no problem, man. I just wanted to make sure Katie was okay. I can't imagine what you're going through. I'm so sorry."

"Yeah, I'm sorry, too," Bradford responds as he exhales and returns to his car.

"Did you tell him his mom was on the tapes?" Nolan asks me once Bradford's car is out of the lot.

"It's not my job to tell him. I'm sure he's headed to the station now, and someone who is a lot more qualified than me in giving bad news will handle it."

I think of Sheriff Nelson and all the bad news he's had to deliver in the last twenty years. I don't know how he does it.

Ten

"**WHAT WOULD** you think about ordering in and watching a movie?" Nolan suggests. "I have an Uber Eats gift card that someone gave me for my birthday last year. We can order whatever you'd like."

I chuckle.

"Oh, sweet Nolan. There is no Uber Eats in the middle of the woods. There also aren't any restaurants that deliver around here other than Johnny's Pizza, and that's only during season. Want to just grab something to go from Benard's?"

He spins around to face the restaurant and claps his hands together once before wrapping his right arm around my shoulders.

"This place? I hadn't even noticed a restaurant here. It's right on the water and looks lovely. Let's go."

"Tone down the sarcasm and I'll talk the night shift into making your fries extra crispy," I promise him while wrapping my arms around his waist and giving a tight squeeze.

"This is the closest thing to a normal date night we're going to get at the moment, so how about we grab some burgers, pick a movie to watch, and leave your ringer on loud so we won't miss any news about Dougie?"

"Sounds like a date." I wink, and he holds the side door to the restaurant open for me.

The dinner rush hasn't started yet so I don't feel too bad about putting in a personal order. Tammy, a woman who has worked part time for the family for over a decade, is behind the bar.

"Hiya, KB. How's Dougie?" she asks, continuing to slice bar fruit as she talks. She doesn't take her eyes off me while retrieving more limes from the stainless-steel bowl in front of her and cutting them into perfect wedges. She's been doing this so long, I'm sure she could make an old fashioned in her sleep.

"No news yet, but thanks for asking. Would you mind putting in two Benard burgers for us? We're going to take it easy tonight and wait for one of the aunts to call."

"You still take your fries extra crispy?" she asks while wiping her hands on the bar towel and leaning over the screen to enter our orders.

I nod. "You betcha."

"And this guy?" she asks, jutting her chin toward Nolan.

"Yes, ma'am," he replies. "I'm Nolan, by the way."

"Nolan, sweetie, I know who you are. I also know you only order your fries crispy when KB is with you because you're worried about seeming like a pain in the ass when you're by yourself."

She doesn't wait for a response before walking away toward the kitchen.

"I'm not afraid to order crispy fries," he says under his breath.

"Oh, Nolan. Sure you are." I smile and reach in my back pocket for a five-dollar bill to leave Tammy. She'll comp our meals under the family discount, but no employee in their right mind stiffs a coworker after they take the time to bag up to-go orders. Nolan also pulls a five out of his wallet and places it on top of mine, tapping it once and nodding. He may not have a service industry background, but he gets it.

We take a seat on two stools near the end of the bar while we wait for our meals. It's always strange to be here as a customer because I can only focus on the things that need to be done. Tammy walked away to check on something in the kitchen, but she didn't fully close the cooler that holds the bar produce. If Lou were here, she'd be throwing a fit about the electric bill. Table twenty-nine is looking around the room for their server because both of their drinks are empty. The couple at the host stand seem okay, but I think the host took a little too long before greeting them. I also know this is because her phone is on a shelf behind the podium, and she was scrolling when they walked in.

"Hey Katie, hey Nolan!"

I turn to my right and see Robbie exiting the kitchen. He's lucky Lou isn't here because she'd have his ass for coming into the dining room wearing his dirty kitchen apron. *I know that prepping food is a dirty job, but the whole damn town doesn't need to know about it. Hang your apron before you leave this kitchen, you animals.*

"I didn't know you were working in the kitchen," I tell him. I know the plan was to find something for him to do until the lake business starts back up, but I didn't realize he had already been assigned somewhere.

"Lou said she could use my help back there this week and maybe a little next week when we prep Thanksgiving orders."

"I cannot believe Thanksgiving is next week. How did this month fly by so fast?" Nolan asks.

"Well, you currently have the top true crime podcast in the country because the disappearance you were investigating turned into a small-town kidnapping ring with several dead bodies and a fugitive or two. Time flies when your life becomes more twisty than a suspense novel, eh?" I intend for my comment to be lighthearted, but Nolan's lips form a straight line as he pulls me into a tight embrace. In fact, the hug is so suffocating that I laugh. "Nolan, what's wrong?"

"I forget sometimes that this is your life, your family, your town. The gravity of what you guys are all going through just hits me sometimes. I know I've made Grady my life because it's been the subject of my investigation the last few months, but I can't imagine how you feel having this chaos surrounding you. I'm sorry if I don't tell you that enough."

"My parents say that Grady has always had its secrets, that they are just all coming to the surface now. Whatever that means," Robbie adds, nonchalantly taking a bite out of an apple left out on the bar, another act that would make Lou's head spin with anger. The apples are to be cut into small circular garnishes for the sangria special this week, and dear Robbie just consumed about ten drinks worth of garnish.

I'm about to question the context of the statement made by Robbie's parents when my phone begins to ring. It catches me off guard. I normally keep it on vibrate but I didn't want to miss a call tonight. My chest tightens when I see the screen display Lou's name and her contact photo in my phone, which is a throwback to her holding a record-weight walleye in one hand and a Busch Light in the other, with a cigarette hanging out of the corner of her mouth. It's my favorite picture of her because the joy on her face is genuine and that didn't happen much after Malorie disappeared.

She begins talking before I can say hello.

"He's awake. He's gonna be alright, kid. He's gonna be alright," she says, and quickly adds her signature snark to cover the emotion in her voice. "Still dumb as a box of rocks as far as we can tell, so I don't think the head injury knocked any sense into him."

I laugh and without warning simultaneously begin to cry. I needed good news. I have been trying to keep my mind off it all day, but I just needed Dougie to be okay. Our family deserves good news.

"What's he saying about Chelsey? Does he know he was drugged?" I ask. Nolan and Robbie's eyes both grow wide at my mention of Dougie being conscious, followed by enormous grins. This makes me burst out in tears again, so I turn my back to them.

"He's in there with Nelson now. We'll find out what he knows shortly, but we don't want to overwhelm him. Don't worry about coming up here tonight. The doc says we need to let him rest. How's about you come up in the morning and bring him one of those stupid donuts he likes?"

The "stupid donuts he likes" are just the individually packed snack cakes from the Grab N Go, but it makes me smile knowing that Lou remembers.

"You got it," I tell her.

"Alright, I'm going to get off here, but tell that damn Robbie if I catch him in the dining room with his dirty kitchen apron again, he's not gonna like it."

She hangs up the phone, and I glance up at the security camera over the bar. Even in the hospital waiting room, Lou is always watching. I spin around to face Nolan and Robbie, who are now joined by Tammy and a neatly packed bag of takeout containers with my name on it.

"The good news is he's awake and seems to be doing okay, other than needing some rest. I'll go see him first thing in the morning. The bad news is Lou said she's going to throat punch you if you don't get out of the dining room with that filthy apron," I say, pointing to Robbie.

He's momentarily confused before lifting his chin and searching the walls for security cameras. He finds the one closest to the bar and waves innocently while taking off his apron and holding it up to the camera, which puts more focus on the dirty garment. I can just picture Lou now, shaking her head while watching the footage on her phone.

"That's the best news ever," Nolan tells me, with a quick side-hug and kiss on the top of my head. "This might be a stress-free date night after all."

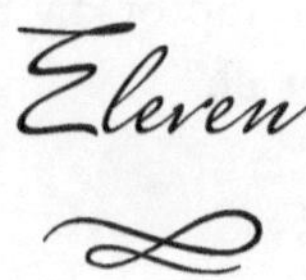

Eleven

WE FINALLY SPENT the night together. Not in the way the mind naturally travels when I say we spent the night together, but we slept under the same roof, in the same bed, and it was glorious.

I didn't, however, plan on staying the night, so I hop out of bed and tiptoe to the bathroom before he can smell my morning breath or get a glimpse of my hair, which I'm sure looks like I've been caught up in an F5 tornado. I ease the door closed behind me and pour cold water into my cupped hands and gargle it, which is the best substitution for brushing my teeth that I can come up with. A few minutes spent finger-combing my unruly hair and patting my face with splashes of water, and I'm ready to face the day and hope Nolan doesn't wake up enough to get a close look at me before I sneak out to go visit Dougie at the hospital.

I pad as quietly as I can over to my shoes, which are next to the front door, where I left them last night. Through the small window next to the entryway, I can see light frost on the grass outside. *Thanksgiving. Next week.*

"You got what you wanted and now you're leaving me?"

Nolan says, his unexpected voice making me jump. He's leaned up on one elbow and has apparently been enjoying watching me attempt to sneak around so I wouldn't wake him. Unlike me, Nolan doesn't need to fix his hair or splash water on his face. The sleep marks on his cheeks are somehow adorable, and his messy brown hair only gives him a look of sweet innocence.

"Yes, that's my M.O.—a night of strictly PG cuddling and I'm out of here. I'm a real heartbreaker." I take a few steps back toward the bed and perch myself on the end.

"I mean, it wasn't *all* PG," he says, quickly leaning forward to pull my body on top of his.

"Stop!" I yell with a laugh. "I haven't brushed my teeth!"

"You have morning breath? That's it, we are done. I never want to see you again, Katie Benard," he tells me before hopping out of bed and picking me up. He lugs me over his shoulder like a sack of potatoes and I'm laughing so hard, I'm afraid I might pee.

He marches over to the door, holding me with one arm while he opens it with the other. He sets me down on the concrete patio outside the cabin and adds, "and don't you ever come back here with that stinky breath again."

I'm startled by a laugh behind me, coming from the cabin next door. Karli's cabin.

"Nicole?" I ask. She's closing the cabin door behind her and is wearing the same outfit she had on yesterday when we drove home from the hospital.

"Um, is Dougie okay? Any word?"

"Oh, were you checking with Karli to see if she knew about Dougie before we did?" I ask, seeing through her attempt to change the focus from her little sleepover.

"That outfit looks familiar; didn't we see you in it yester-day?" Nolan adds.

We both stand with our arms crossed, wearing smug grins.

She's been caught, and she has no reasonable explanation for why she's leaving Karli's cabin at seven in the morning.

"Well, you see, what happened was—"

She's interrupted by Karli popping out of the door behind her, a cup of steaming coffee in her hand and a plush navy-blue bathrobe wrapped around her body.

"*What happened was* I've been working my ass off for years while my wife was cheating on me, and I decided to do something for myself for once. That's what happened. I've only been with one woman for the last eight years, and it was time to broaden my horizons."

I can't help myself. "And you decided to broaden your horizons with . . . Nicole?"

"Fuck you, KB," Nicole replies. "Don't listen to her; she's just jealous," she says to Karli.

"Hey, we're not here to judge," I respond smugly.

"Like hell we're not," Nolan counters. "In fact, we're going back in the cabin to talk about you guys." He grabs my hand, winks at our two best friends, and pulls me back inside his rental.

"Wait, what about Dougie?" Nicole yells. When I don't answer, she lets herself into the cabin behind us, pulling me into one of her stupid headlocks.

"He's fine, he's going to be fine, let me go!"

"Damn, Nolan, you were right. Her breath is *kickin'*," she tells him, rubbing my scalp with her knuckles a few times before releasing me.

"I can't stand you," I remind her.

"I can't stand you, either. Want to grab coffee and head up to the hospital?" she asks me.

"Fine. But I'm driving."

* * *

By the time I'm taking the exit for the hospital, which I've become entirely too familiar with, I'm officially caught up on Nic's budding relationship, which began when Karli received a call from a friend back home giving her the unfortunate news that her wife had, in fact, been cheating for the entirety of their marriage. Nicole saw the familiar signs of a woman who was about to lose it, so she quickly swooped in and distracted her with a late fall hike in the Hiawatha Forest, a discussion about her favorite movies, and a homecooked dinner in her rented cabin. Knowing Nicole as well as I do, she had good intentions, but I'm certain she was also keenly aware of how the night would most likely end after lending a shoulder to cry on and cooking chicken marsala.

"So, did he take his khaki pants off while you made love or just unzip them enough to get the job done?" she asks as we pull in the parking lot. I reach over and punch her hard in the shoulder, which results in her doing the same to me and then having to call a truce when I need to focus on parking my car between the lines.

"He slept in grey sweatpants, but we didn't hook up. I'm sorry to disappoint you."

Once the car is in park, she hits my arm one more time for good measure.

"Straight girls do love gray sweatpants. He knew what he was doing," she tells me, reaching over to unbuckle her seatbelt and grab the snack cakes from the back seat. I giggle, thinking of Nolan making any sort of calculated move to attract me. He's a lot of things, but suave isn't one of them. It was just a happy accident that he grabbed gray sweatpants from his pile of clean laundry . . . I think.

When we are walking through the main entrance of the hospital, my phone vibrates with a text from Lou. Deb and Mal are in the room with Dougie, and Lou and Brenda are headed back to Benard's to get the restaurant open for lunch service. She's going to tell Brenda about her ex-husband on the way over.

"Text me if she has a nervous breakdown and I have to come work her shift," I respond.

"Might want to keep that phone on ya, kid," Lou says, and I smile. Sure, Brenda will have legitimate reason to lose her shit when she gets the news about Dennis, but it's still fun to have this back-and-forth with Lou about it.

Nicole and I head up to the third floor while she berates me for choosing the elevator instead of the stairs.

"See, this is what's wrong with your generation. You're soft," she tells me as the doors open with a ding.

"We're the same age, dumbass."

"Are you two really fighting at a time like this?"

We both turn to find Aunt Deb sitting in a chair outside Dougie's room, working on a knitting project.

"*A time like this*? I thought he was going to be fine?" Nicole asks.

Deb purses her lips and sets the knitting needles in her lap, a small ball of yarn tumbling to her feet.

"Physically he is fine, but I'm sure the trauma of being attacked by someone he thought he loved will haunt him forever, Nicole."

I squeeze Nicole's arm to prevent her from tossing sarcasm at my sweet aunt, and thankfully, she abides.

"You're absolutely right, Aunt Deb. We will support him however we can while he recovers. Is he up for guests?" I ask.

She nods. "Mal just ran down to the cafeteria to grab something to eat. Dougie is resting, but I'm sure he'd be happy to see you both."

"Thanks, Deb. That's a beautiful blanket you've started," I tell her, pointing at the few rows of tightly stitched baby-blue yarn.

"It's a scarf, for Douglas."

This time I use a death grip on Nicole's arm to stop her from whatever it is that's about to spew out of her mouth. She works so hard to control her laughter, a humming sound comes from her mouth, and she bites down, sucking her lips in. "That's really sweet, Deb; he's going to be nice and warm this winter," she manages to say before we disappear into Dougie's room.

We close the door behind us, and luckily, Dougie is alert and sitting up in his bed, holding a cup of pudding in one hand and a spoon in the other. Without hesitation, Nicole walks over to Dougie, motions for him to scoot over, and climbs into bed next to him. She lifts several tubes and wires that are attached to him with ease, like she invites herself into hospital beds regularly. She kicks her Converse sneakers onto the floor, reaches across Dougie for the remote, and begins channel surfing.

"Just make yourself at home, Nic," Dougie tells her, setting the pudding down on the tray table and throwing his arms in the air in mock frustration.

Nicole sets the remote in her lap and slowly turns toward Dougie, staring in his eyes for a few seconds before speaking.

"Heard you got knocked the fuck out."

Her smile spreads like the Cheshire cat. Dougie huffs and turns his attention to me.

"KB, why did you let her come? You knew she was going to be like this."

Nicole reaches her hand out in my direction, wanting the snack cakes she handed to me in the elevator. I toss them to her before making my way to Dougie's side of the bed and gently hugging him, careful not to squeeze too hard.

"I love you, Doug. We were really worried about you. Whether she admits it or not, so was Nicole."

He hugs me back, which may be the first physical contact we've had—other than punching each other—in years.

"I wasn't worried," Nicole mumbles. "We brought you these."

Dougie takes one of the cakes out of her hand and unwraps the plastic, biting off half of the dessert and sprinkling a trail of crumbs over the front of his hospital gown and blanket.

"I love you guys," he says, wiping his mouth with the back of his hand. "I've been awake for less than a day and I'm already sick of the food here."

"Do you want to talk about it?" Nicole asks. I begin to interject, but Dougie holds his hand up to stop me.

"There's not a whole lot to say. She was involved with Palmer. I found Polaroids in her cabin, but she must have taken them with her when she left because Nelson said they haven't located them. I don't remember much, but I started to feel nauseous just like I did after the birthday party. I think she drugged me both times; I just don't know what her motive was the night of the party, because I didn't know anything at that point."

"What were the Polaroids of?" I ask, regretting the question the minute the words leave my lips.

He stares forward, focused on the foot of the bed for a beat before replying, "You don't even want to know. Let's just say they better fucking find her."

"I'm so sorry. I know you liked her," Nicole says.

"With your dad, we were all fooled. Sure, he was quiet and kind of an asshole, but none of us knew he was a monster. With Chelsey, I had a strange feeling around her. I liked her a lot, so I ignored it, but I should have listened to my gut," he tells Nicole, who flinches slightly at the mention of her dad.

"They're going to find her," I tell him, hoping it's the truth.

We all turn when Mal walks in the room with an armful of snacks from the vending machine. She dumps them out on the foot of the bed, and Nicole hesitantly grabs a bag of chips before thanking Mal. She's still not sure where they stand, so she's been on her best behavior.

"It occurred to me when I was walking the halls of the hospital that I think this is my first time being alone outside of the lodge since I came home," Mal tells us. She's not looking at any of us, just staring wide-eyed at the pile of snacks she purchased. "It was really liberating."

"Did you feel safe? Did anyone bother you?" I ask, suddenly aware of how irresponsible it was for Deb to send Mal down there by herself. Deb is the queen of being overly cautious. I can't believe I didn't panic when she told us that Mal ran to the cafeteria; I guess I was just too focused on seeing Dougie.

"Calm down, you sound like Deb. Nobody even looked at me twice. You guys are going to have to let me live my life sooner or later; I'm damn near forty years old."

I've worried about my big sister every day for the last twenty years. I don't anticipate that changing any time soon, but I'll do my best to help her feel normal. Maybe I'll just start worrying from a safe distance.

"Nic, if you don't mind, would you excuse us for a minute? I think we need to have a little family meeting and discuss some things with Dougie," I say, nodding to Mal so she's on the same page. I had just pulled my phone out of my pocket to a text from Lou saying that it went okay with Brenda, but she'd like Mal and I to be the ones who tell Dougie about his dad. She's going to watch the restaurant so Brenda can drive up to the hospital after the lunch rush and have some alone time with him so they can process the news.

"No, whatever you need to say, Nicole can hear it. She's family," Dougie says and nudges Nicole, who is still sitting next to him in the bed.

"It's really okay, guys," she says, swinging her legs off the side and onto the tile floor.

"I agree, she should stay," Mal says, and I try not to show my initial surprise at her declaration. Dougie doesn't know about the conflict between Nic and my sister, which means he has no idea of the gravity of that statement.

Nicole nods and climbs back in bed without a word. I have a feeling it's because she'd lose it if she opened her mouth. I cannot imagine the relief she's feeling. I walk behind Mal and close the hospital door so we aren't overheard by any onlookers.

"Doug, we love you and this is going to be hard to hear," I begin.

"Rip it off like a band-aid, KB. Just say it," he says, bottom lip quivering. The last twenty-four hours really has toughened him up.

"Yesterday Lieutenant Barkley from the state police asked Mal, Lou, and me to come down to the station and watch some footage from Rich's trail cams that were pointed on the bunkers. He's had a series of cameras there for years, going back to before Mal was even taken."

Nicole once again flinches at the mention of her father, but we filled her in on the tapes yesterday when she and my dad arrived in the waiting room, so this isn't a total shock for her.

"It appears, years ago that Lincoln Palmer had two accomplices working with him to kidnap the girls and transport them to the property. They each only appear on the tapes once, so the detectives aren't sure of the extent of their involvement. The first one was his ex-wife, JoAnne, and the second one was your dad, Dougie. I'm so fucking sorry."

He stares at me for a moment before speaking.

"Dennis? Dennis was on the tapes? You're sure?"

Dougie hasn't called him "Dad" since we were little. Dennis lost the privilege of that title a long time ago.

"We're sure," Mal chimes in.

"Does Mom know?"

"Lou just told her. She needs a little time to process, and then she's going to head up here so you guys can have some alone time," I tell him. This is news to Mal and Nicole, who I'm sure have been waiting to hear how it went with Lou and Brenda.

"Is that why he left town for good? Is that why he hasn't visited? Because he didn't want to get arrested?" Dougie asks, his rapidly darting eyes putting together the pieces of his father's absence.

"I don't know, Dougie. We don't know much yet. Has he mentioned where he's staying? I know it's a shitty position to be in, but it looks like he did some horrible things, and we need to make sure he is held accountable," I tell him.

Dougie shakes his head rapidly. "No, it's not a shitty position to be in. It's a great position to be in, that I could put him behind bars where he belongs. He hasn't been a dad to me in a long fucking time. I haven't heard from him since my last birthday, but he said he was in Orlando. Working some construction job, but I'm sure he's getting paid under the table."

"Okay, we'll tell Nelson so he can look into it. Anything else you remember that could help find him?" I ask.

"Nelson? Nelson knows? He just questioned me all morning about Chelsey and didn't say a word about it."

"Lou asked him to let the family break the news to you because you've been through enough the last twenty-four hours. Benefit of a small town, I guess," I say.

My phone once again vibrates, and it's Lou telling me that Brenda is heading up a little early because she wants to see

Dougie. I tell her that Nic and I will head back and help out at the restaurant.

"Your mom is on her way up here, so we'll give you a little peace and quiet to gather your thoughts. Whatever you need, Dougie. You just let us know, okay?"

He silently nods, and we take turns giving him gentle hugs as we prepare to leave. Just as my hand touches the door handle to open it, he says, "Wait," and we all turn in unison. He's staring at Nicole.

"How did you handle it, finding out your dad is a fucking monster? How do you live with that?" he asks.

"I still don't know, Dougie. But I'll let you know if I ever figure it out," she says before leaving the room.

Twelve

MAL IS WAKING up as I stumble out of our en-suite bathroom, still feeling half asleep. I pull a pair of fuzzy socks out of my dresser because the floors are freezing, and my slippers are nowhere in sight. She shivers and pulls her comforter up to her chin before moaning, "Why can't Lou let us turn the heat on like a normal family?"

"Oh, she's got it on. She just refuses to turn it above sixty-five degrees until we have serious snowfall. She's a monster," I reply. I open my closet and grab two sweatshirts, throwing one to my sister.

Opening our bedroom door, I'm relieved to smell a fresh pot of coffee brewing. I know Brenda and Deb were scheduled to do morning prep at the restaurant, which means Lou must be responsible. After hearing the unmistakable squeak of our door hinge—another thing that needs to be fixed but keeps moving down the to-do list—Lou calls out to us.

"Katie, Mal, come out here and look at this."

Mal scrunches her nose before hopping out of bed to join me. I throw a second pair of fuzzy socks her way, knowing she'll need them because the family room with its tall ceilings and large windows is typically colder than our tiny, insulated room.

When we turn the corner to enter the family room, Lou is standing in front of the TV with her arms folded. It's not local news she's watching, it's national. JoAnne Palmer is being led into a building by two officers with her hands cuffed in front of her body. The caption on the bottom of the screen reads MILLIONAIRE'S EX-WIFE ARRESTED IN CONNECTION TO THE BUNKERS OF HORROR CASE IN MICHIGAN.

The cameras cut to Sheriff Nelson standing at a podium in a room I don't recognize. As they pan away, I see the location tag beneath his name on the screen says Marquette, Michigan. Maybe he is making a conscious effort to drive attention *away* from our little town for once.

The three of us watch silently as Nelson reads from a printed piece of paper in his hands. He gives the basic evidence that led to JoAnne's arrest, as well as mentioning two other suspects on the bunker tapes who are currently at large. Uncle Dennis and Chelsey's photos pop up on the screen, with a phone number to call if the public has any information on either suspect.

"I've lived in Grady my entire life. Until 2003, it was a sleepy little town where a whole lot of nothing happened. I'd sincerely like to get back to that way of life as soon as possible for myself and the other residents of Grady, but that cannot happen until both Dennis Coleman and Chelsey Benoit are apprehended and prosecuted for their crimes."

Lou's head swivels in my direction, confirming that I'm not mistaken. He said Chelsey Benoit.

"What? What's wrong?" Mal asks.

"Benoit . . . that was my fiancé's last name. Dave Benoit. The guy who cheated on me," I answer.

"I'm sure it's just a coincidence. I've met a few Benoits in my day," Lou assures me, but I know her well enough to know she's lying.

"I saw her application for the restaurant. That's not the last name she used. I think it was Pritchard," I say. "Why else would she hide her last name if she has no connection to Dave? What other reason would she have?"

"I don't know, kid. Maybe she had a bad divorce or something. I'll give Nelson a few minutes to finish up his conference and get on the road, and then I'll give him a call. If there's any connection to Dave, we'll find out."

"Did you meet his family?" Malorie asks, and my stomach cramps when I realize where she's going with this.

"He didn't have a great relationship with his parents. They were always calling and asking us to come home for the holidays, but he always had a million excuses why he didn't want to go."

Lou calmly asks the question that's on all our minds.

"Katie, did he have any siblings?"

I don't know why I'm ashamed to answer. It's not like I personally did anything wrong. Yet, my voice goes up a few octaves when I respond, "Yes, a sister. No, I never met her. He said she traveled a lot for her job, so he hadn't seen her in over a year."

"Well . . . was her name Chelsey?" Mal asks.

Again, I'm ashamed to answer. "It was C.J. but I never asked what it stood for."

Why didn't I ask more questions? Why didn't I insist on meeting his family before I accepted his proposal? The thought of Chelsey being his sister is too much to bear. He came up here a few times with me for long weekends and acted like he had no knowledge of Grady Lake before he met me. Is it possible his sister was staying across the lake, working for Lincoln Palmer, and Dave didn't know? Or did he know, and he was keeping it from me? It's too crazy to even think about.

I'm overreacting. Benoit is not the most unique name in the world. It's entirely possible they have no connection.

I scramble for my phone to check Dave's Facebook page. I navigate to the search bar with shaking hands. No results. Either he got rid of social media or, more likely, he has me blocked. He was just begging me for another chance weeks ago; what a change of heart he must have had. I try my luck at searching Chelsey Benoit but there aren't any results for profiles, only news stories about the blonde-haired fugitive. I'm focusing intently on the screen, reading one of the articles, when my phone starts vibrating with a call from Nolan, nearly causing me to drop it.

"Hey," I answer, turning from Lou and Mal and walking into the kitchen for some privacy.

"Did you see they caught Palmer's ex?" he asks. I tell him everything—about how we broke the news to Dougie and Brenda about Dennis, about how Chelsey has the same last name as my ex-fiancé and it's probably nothing, but Lou is going to mention it to Nelson.

"I've got a guy. I can have an answer for you this morning," he tells me.

"You've *got a guy*? What does that even mean?" I ask.

"We do a lot of fact checking in my business. I've got a guy whose job is to verify things. I can find out if they are related. Give me like an hour."

"I'm not sure if your guy has any resources that the Michigan State Police don't already have, but if you could have him look into Dennis Coleman's whereabouts as well, that would be amazing," I suggest.

With this, Lou swings toward me and raises her eyebrows.

"You got it," he replies before ending the call.

"You think this kid could find Dennis?" Lou asks.

"I'm not sure, but it's worth a try," I say.

"I agree with Nelson. I think we all just want our lives to

get back to normal. Or, as normal as things can get in this family," Mal says, gesturing to the TV, where the sheriff is answering questions from the press.

We all freeze at the mention of Malorie's name.

"Sheriff, have there been any developments in the search for the remains of Malorie Benard's deceased child?" a reporter shouts.

"We will announce any developments in that case as we have them. In the meantime, we ask that you journalists try something new and give that poor family some privacy."

Thirteen

BY THE NEXT DAY, Dougie is discharged from the hospital, but not without a little unwelcome fanfare. Brenda said they were approached several times outside the hospital doors for comment, and she's certain they were followed by a black sedan all the way back to the lake. Tammy, who is opening the restaurant today, says there are several reporters camped out waiting for a sighting of any member of the Benard family. We are trusting the employees to run the place today while we hide out at the lodge, which has become an all-too-common plan after news breaks.

Malorie is lying down with another one of her headaches, and Lou is out on the balcony chain smoking and staring daggers at any customers gathered in the parking lot who she suspects might be journalists. *It's nearing the end of November. Real customers get their asses inside where it's warm and eat their dinner. They aren't lingering around playing grab-ass like a bunch of yahoos. If they're outside, they're one of them.*

Deb and I are waiting on the couch for Brenda to emerge from Dougie's bedroom, where she is tucking him in for an afternoon nap like a five-year-old. Just as she comes out and carefully closes the door behind her, Lou comes in through the patio doors to announce that Sheriff Nelson will be at the lodge in an hour to give us all an update on the investigations. Plural—*investigations*—because we now have one new arrest and two fugitives to add to our family nightmare that won't seem to end.

"I'm so embarrassed that I didn't see it. Dennis was an asshole, but I never dreamed he was also a predator. I feel so foolish," Brenda says before taking a seat on the couch next to me and cradling her head in her hands.

"A whole lot of assholes around here have been living double lives that we knew nothing about. It's not time to start feeling sorry for ourselves because we didn't see it sooner," Lou grumbles.

"This whole ordeal is just making me sick. I swear I've had a stomachache for a month straight," Deb adds, wrapping one arm around her midsection to emphasize her claim.

"As soon as they track down Chelsey and Dennis, we can try to act like a normal family again. I don't think there will be anyone left to commit any crimes once they're arrested, and I wish that was a joke," I say while wondering if we'll ever really experience normal again.

Our bedroom door creaks open, and Mal walks quietly down the hallway with a throw blanket wrapped around her shoulders to join us in the family room.

"Twenty years trapped in a room and now I'm trapped in this lodge. I never thought I'd say this, but I can't wait until it's safe for me to work at Benard's again. I just need a change of scenery and a little human interaction," Mal tells us.

Thinking of the reasons Mal *can't* work at the resort yet infuriates me. All she wants to do is sell gas to the boaters or serve burgers to the locals so she can get out of this house, but the nosey jerks of the world are going to make that impossible for her. Due to no fault of her own, Mal may never be able to live a normal life again.

"Once this nonsense dies down, we could put you in the kitchen for a few hours a week. I know it's not what you want, but it would get you out of the house and allow you to have a conversation with someone outside this family. I'm sure the employees who knew you as a kid would love to see ya," Lou tells her.

"Speaking of having conversations with people outside this family . . ." We all turn to look at Mal. She doesn't have a cell phone, and other than running down to the cafeteria at the hospital, we haven't let her out of our sights for a minute. "I think I might be ready to see my high school friends. Well, at least the ones who were in my close circle," she says, turning to me. "Are Anna, Taylor, or Cassie still around?"

I smile. I've been waiting for this moment to come. Mal's therapist Dalia told me not to initiate the conversation or attempt to force any interactions on her until she's ready. When Mal wasn't with me or working at Benard's, she was typically with those three girls when we were young. They did everything together.

"We've been keeping in contact since you were found. I give them updates when I can, but they are all dying to see you. Anna lives downstate in Alpena, Taylor is just up the road in Marquette, and Cassie is in Escanaba with her parents. Whenever you're ready, I can group text them and set something up."

"Do they . . . have children? Are they married?" she asks, forcing a smile that breaks my heart in two.

I match it with an equally artificial dose of positivity as I answer her. "Anna has two little boys and married her college sweetheart. Taylor is divorced with a twelve-year-old daughter, and Cassie never married or had kids. She's a traveling nurse and just happens to be back in Michigan, so she's holding off on taking another contract until she can see you."

Mal nods as I'm speaking, though I cannot imagine what is going through her mind. Her friends lived entire lives in the twenty years she was locked in Rich's basement.

Our conversation is cut short by a knock at the door, presumably Nelson with his promised updates for the family. Brenda hops up since she's closest to the door and opens it to reveal not only Nelson but two of his officers standing behind him on the landing. He nods to them both, motioning to stay put before he enters. I'm confused—does my family suddenly require the presence of armed guards outside our lodge door?

"Hello, ladies. I trust Douglas made it home safely from Marquette?" he asks, setting his hat on the kitchen island before walking across the floor of the family room and taking a seat in one of the recliners facing the center of the room.

"He's feeling much better today, Sheriff. Thank you," Brenda says as she retakes her place on the couch next to me.

Nelson checks his watch, pulls his cell phone off its waistband clip, and nods to himself. "Ladies, Nolan Cowell, who I'm sure you're familiar with," he begins, jutting his chin in my direction as he says it, "is about to arrive here at the lodge. He stopped to see me this afternoon with some information he obtained through one of his resources from the podcast, and I have to say, it's good work. He was able to get some answers faster than we could even get MSP to start looking. I felt it was only fair that he be present with the family as we tell you what we've learned in the last twenty-four hours."

I scrunch my nose at the news—Nolan is on his way here and hasn't even contacted me to let me know he found something? I then remember that I'm not wearing my smart watch and haven't looked at my phone in hours, so I sheepishly stand up to retrieve it from the kitchen. Sure enough, there are several texts from Nolan, letting me know that he has news and he's coming to tell me in person. I guess I'm the asshole once again.

"I'm sure you ladies have heard by now that JoAnne was arrested outside her home in lower Michigan. I have a phone conference with the investigators down there, but early indications are that she's going to talk. I don't believe her participation with Lincoln lasted long, but there's no doubt that she was involved at least temporarily with his crimes," Nelson tells us.

"Will they cut a deal with her, even if her testimony can't help prosecutors because Lincoln is dead?" I ask.

"It all depends on the information she has. If she can help provide testimony on the involvement of any of the other suspects, or lead us to any remains we haven't already discovered, I wouldn't be surprised if prosecutors cut a deal with her. Other than her involvement with her ex-husband, she's been a law-abiding citizen. She doesn't have so much as a speeding ticket on her record in the last decade."

I'm dying to know what she will say in her defense. Was she afraid of Lincoln? Why didn't she go to authorities after they divorced? Did he threaten her or pay her off? It's hard to put a dollar amount on silence when it involves the kidnapping of teenage girls. There isn't enough money in this world that would keep my mouth shut if I knew someone was doing what he did.

One of the officers standing guard outside on the landing —and I'm still not sure why they are here—gives a tap on the door before opening it and allowing Nolan to enter. He doesn't seem at all fazed by their presence. I'm not sure if I should hug him in front of everyone, especially since this is a serious occasion, so I just scoot over on the couch and make room for him to sit with Brenda and me.

"Although the MSP were quick to put a trace on Chelsey's cell phone and the last few numbers that Dennis used to text Douglas, Nolan and his associate put together some pieces for us on the personal lives of both fugitives," Nelson tells us and gives Nolan a tight smile. "Chelsey Benoit's cell phone pinged in Grady just two days ago and hasn't been used since. We have an Attempt to Locate out on her with highway patrols in all neighboring states. None of the prepaid phones that Dennis Coleman used to contact his son are in use anymore, but we do have some interesting information. Last year, when he texted Douglas on his birthday, the phone was used in Marquette. We are looking to get call records on the numbers, but it's next to impossible with these prepaid phones."

Nelson motions for Nolan to take over and everyone's focus shifts to him. Although he's very well-spoken, he's also used to speaking alone and behind a microphone, so I know the attention is making him uneasy.

"My contact was able to trace Dennis' location in 2004 through 2006 to a small town in central Florida where he was working a construction job, but that's the last time his name or social security number were used for a W-2. I know it's frustrating, but it's also entirely common in that industry to work for cash under the table. If Dennis didn't need a home loan or any other financing that required proof of income, it's not too far-fetched to think he works solely for cash, so he doesn't pay taxes."

"Sounds about right for that piece of shit," Lou says and immediately raises her hands in apology to Brenda. Although Brenda wouldn't have framed it so harshly, her casual shrug says she doesn't exactly disagree with her older sister.

"We've contacted the local police department in Eatonville, which was his last known location. They're going to ask around and show Dennis' picture to see what they can find out, but with all the undocumented workers on the construction sites down there, it's not very likely they'll talk to a cop. We're going to stay cautiously optimistic about getting answers," Nelson tells us.

Nolan's right heel is tapping on the carpet, and he's wiping the sweat off his hands by rubbing his palms on the knees of his jeans. I wish Nicole was here to see he's not wearing khakis. I'm surprised that talking to my family is making him this nervous.

"Chelsey's background was a little more difficult because she's used several aliases for work," Nolan begins, "especially while working for small family-owned businesses, which typically don't run background checks." I'm not sure why I feel a pang of guilt when he says this. It's the Upper Peninsula of Michigan; we've never *needed* to run background checks on our employees. Most of them are classmates of ours or relatives of other employees. The thought has never crossed my mind to run their names through any sort of system.

"I know Katie was particularly curious when she heard Chelsey's real surname used on the news, since her former fiancé was also a Benoit," he says, avoiding eye contact with me. He's never been uncomfortable talking to me about Dave. This is so strange.

"My source confirmed today that Chelsey *is* related to Dave Benoit. But, she's not his sister . . . she's his wife."

Fourteen

SHE'S WEARING MY RING. She's wearing my fucking engagement ring. I'm staring at a photo of Dave and Chelsey *on their honeymoon*, and she has my solitaire engagement ring with rose gold accents that Dave swore he designed himself. My heart would flutter each time he'd tell the story of visiting the local jeweler down the street from our rental in Lansing, and that he'd had to go back a handful of times until it was *just right*. On the days I doubted if Dave was the one for me because I was getting my typical cold feet about the relationship, I'd remind myself how lucky I was to have a man who cared enough to personally design the ring he gave me. How is this happening?

Although Nolan's hand is lightly touching my back, nobody is speaking to me. I'm sure none of them know what the hell to even say. I left the man because he cheated on me, but it turns out he was cheating with us both because he had a wife. I *lived* with Dave full time for the last year or so of our relationship. How did he carry on having a wife for an entire year without coming "home" to her?

"Were they . . . separated?" I ask.

"We're still trying to figure out the dynamic between them, but yes, I think it's safe to say they were separated. They were married in 2008 and have yet to file a divorce petition. No children that we've found," Nolan answers. I cannot fathom how strange this conversation must be for him.

He flips through his phone to another photograph of Dave and Chelsey—this one of their wedding. Next to Dave is his best friend, Mike. Mike, who I have met a thousand times. Mike, who lied to my face each time. I distinctly recall a night at a local wing and beer restaurant in Lansing where Mike had a few too many and tearfully told me how Dave had *never* felt this way about another woman and how happy he was that his best friend had *finally* found love. What a crock of shit.

"So, what's the motive here? Dave sends Chelsey up here to ruin our family's lives? I don't understand why he'd do that. Katie didn't wrong him; he's the one who cheated on her," Lou says. She's now walking back and forth behind Nelson's chair. She won't smoke in the house, but she does have a pack of cigarettes in one hand and her lighter in the other, so the thought has certainly crossed her mind.

Nelson coughs briefly and turns his head to Lou, who stops her frantic pacing to focus on him. "Well, Chelsey has been at the lake for well over a year. If she had any intention of harming Katie or any other member of your family, it would be in retribution for Katie sleeping with her husband, not a mission she was sent to complete by him. At least that would be my best educated guess with the information we have. I feel that I also need to tell you the reason I was surprised you hired Chelsey in the first place. I caught her sneaking around the resort several times last year, but I just chased her off, assuming she was doing a little recon for her employer."

This news is like a slap in the face. How could I be so foolish? This entire conversation had me wracking my brain for reasons Dave and Chelsey would want to hurt my family. It not once occurred to me that Chelsey came up here on her own for retribution since I was *the other woman*. There is a good chance Dave doesn't know anything about this. Was she sneaking around the resort looking for me, or just more information on my family?

"When I heard they were married, my mind instantly flew to them working together. He has lied to me so many times, I wouldn't put it past him to have some nefarious plan with his secret wife," I say, staring at the floor in front of me.

"Well, you've only known that you were the mistress for all of five minutes. I think it's going to take a little while longer before all the pieces make sense here," Mal adds, trying to be helpful. When she was taken, I was a naïve fifteen-year-old. She's been back for a month, and now she's having to hear about how I was in love with a married man. I'm sure this is just as surreal for her as it is for me.

My phone, which I retrieved from the kitchen after Nelson arrived, begins to vibrate in my hand. "Oh my god, it's him," I say. "I have Dave's number blocked, but he's calling from his office."

Nearly everyone in the room shouts some version of "Answer it!" and I hold one finger to my mouth to hush them before I accept it and immediately click the speakerphone button.

"What do you want?" I answer with the same hostility I've shown him the last few times he's tried to contact me. Mal pumps a proud fist in the air.

"I just heard about Dougie. Kate, the girl who attacked him is my ex-wife. I don't know what the hell she is doing in Grady of all places. My head is spinning. I nearly passed out when I saw her picture on the news."

I exhale for a few seconds before speaking because it tends to stop me from word vomiting all over with the hateful things I'd like to say but would not be beneficial for anyone involved. "Ex-wife? That's funny; I just heard from a team of investigators that you're still married. Not only that, but you were married the entire time we were engaged."

I know the silence all too well. He's trying to think of a lie. I cannot believe I dealt with his shit for so long.

"We just never got around to finalizing the divorce. She was always traveling, and it was hard to get her to sign the paperwork because I never knew her latest phone number or address. I swear I was going to get it taken care of before we got married," he says with a pleading voice. I'm not sure why he's putting so much effort into convincing me. I don't give a shit what he says.

"Before we got married with the ring you designed especially for me?" I say, with more vitriol in my voice than I knew possible. Mal, once again, is over the moon with my performance, and Lou is nodding her head in approval.

"I had just finished grad school, Kate. I didn't have a lot of money, but I couldn't wait to propose to you, so I used a stupid old ring that wasn't being used anymore. I'm sorry."

Well, he's learned to apologize. That's new.

"Look, Dave. Not only did you cheat on me, lie about being married, and give me a ring you bought for someone else, but your estranged wife nearly killed my only cousin. You'll have to forgive me if I'm not exactly in the mood to chat. I'd probably keep your phone close, though. I'm sure the investigators have a lot of questions for you *and your wife*."

"You have to believe me," he pleads.

"I don't have to do shit, Dave. Have a nice life," I say, hanging up the phone. Everyone applauds, even Sheriff Nelson, which I'm sure isn't a professional move, but I welcome it.

"I'll make sure the officers in Lansing pay him a visit and scope out his home in case she shows up there," Nelson adds. "Again, nice work Mr. Cowell."

Nelson stands to shake Nolan's hand.

"It was nothing; I just knew who to call. I wish I could have found more on Dennis, but we'll keep looking."

"I know the family appreciates your help, son. And speaking of the family," Nelson says, looking around the room at us remaining Benards, "I'm keeping two officers at the lodge around the clock for the next few days, or at least until we track down Chelsey Benoit. I'm not entirely sure of her motives, but I'd like to catch her before she tries to carry out any more diabolical plans."

Fifteen

NOTHING COULD HAVE PREPARED me for the emotional mess I'd become while witnessing Malorie reunite with her high school best friends for the first time in twenty years.

We closed off the lounge area of the lodge downstairs—where guests of the resort typically can come to play board games, watch DVDs from the 1990s, or sit by the fire—to give Mal and her friends some privacy. They must have been just as nervous as she was because all three of them arrived together. I left Mal on one of the couches so she could have a quiet moment to prepare herself as I stood by the door waiting for the girls to pull in. I say *girls* because I haven't known them since high school, but I suppose we are all women now.

Right at the agreed upon time, a maroon SUV pulls into the Benard's parking lot, and Anna, Taylor, and Cassie emerge. When I open the back door to greet them, all three already have glistening eyes.

"Can we hug her?" Cassie whispers to me after we all lightly embrace each other.

"Of course," I whisper back, hoping that is the correct

answer. I usually take Dalia's advice on these situations, but I forgot to ask about hugging. I'll stay close in case Mal looks like she needs saving.

The women follow me down the narrow hall to the lounge, and I turn back once to give them all an encouraging smile before opening the door. Not only did I tape a Do Not Disturb sign on the outside, but sweet Mable, working the front desk, has agreed to pass along the message to any guests entering the lodge.

Mal rises from her spot on the couch, and her friends don't hesitate—they run to her, the three of them wrapping their arms tightly around her. All I can hear is incoherent ramblings between the sobs, coming from each of them about how much they missed her and how happy they are that she's okay. For what seems like several minutes, nobody lets go. I'm standing a few feet away watching the interaction, and I don't realize how hard I'm crying until drops begin to hit my arms, which are crossed over my chest.

The women pull away to get a good look at Malorie. Although a grainy picture of her leaving the hospital was published on the cover of every magazine in America, nobody has gotten a great look at Mal as an adult. Anna is blotting her face with a tissue while also handing one to Malorie for the same reason. Taylor's hand is pulling the wet strands of Mal's hair from her forehead. Cassie is just awestruck, staring into the eyes of her long-lost friend.

"I'm sorry it took me so long to see you guys . . . I just needed some time," Mal says as they all take seats on the sectional couch.

"Don't you dare apologize," Anna says. "We knew we'd have to wait for you to be ready. We just missed you so damn much."

"We thought we lost you," Taylor adds.

Again, the tears begin to fall. I grab a full tissue box from one of the tables by the door and set it on the couch between Mal and Anna.

"So, tell me everything," Mal says to them after wiping her face, which is now red and splotchy.

"I'm going upstairs to give you some privacy. I'll come back in an hour. Sound good?" I say, backing away from the group of friends.

"Thanks, Katie Bug," Cassie says, the nickname flowing from her lips like it hasn't been twenty years since she last said it to me.

I think this is the first time since Mal came back that I've felt good about letting her out of my sights for a little while. They may not be family, but she's in the presence of three women who love her like she's part of theirs.

* * *

"A thin crust pepperoni with extra cheese from Johnny's would be amazing . . . Maybe one of those flavored ginger ale cans from the Grab N Go?"

Nicole and I are sitting at the foot of Dougie's bed and if we rolled our eyes any harder, they would fly out of their sockets.

"I'm sorry, did Chelsey also break your legs?" she asks him.

"Why did they discharge you from the hospital if you can't perform basic tasks?" I add.

He's preparing his argument when he realizes we are messing with him.

"Do you want fries, princess?" Nicole asks as we are leaving his room.

"I mean . . . I wouldn't turn them down," he answers with a smile. Nicole responds with a middle finger before closing the door behind us.

We're jogging down the back entry stairs of the lodge when she asks how things went with Malorie and her friends.

"Well, she's taking a nap, so I think she's exhausted from the interaction, but I also think it went well. It was really sweet to see them all together again."

"When do you think she'll start going out on her own to do things?" Nicole asks me while we head toward the trail to the Grab N Go. I texted my order into Johnny himself before we left, so it should be ready after we grab a few cans of ginger ale from Nic's store.

"I don't really have an answer to that. Mal feeling like she can leave the house alone is one thing, but convincing Lou that it's a good idea is another."

We walk in silence for a few steps before I notice Nicole wiping her eye quickly and rubbing the back of that hand on her jeans.

"I'm so sorry for what my dad took from your family," she says quietly.

"Nic, we've been through this. It had nothing to do with you, and you have nothing to apologize for. We can't control the actions of our relatives. You think I'd choose for Dougie to be the way he is?"

This thankfully gets a quick laugh, and I wrap my arms around her as we scurry down the trail, the late November chill in full effect.

"Is Khaki Pants going to come to the Moose with us tonight?" she asks.

With everything going on, I nearly forgot about tonight. The night before Thanksgiving is one of The Moose Trap's busiest nights because all the college kids and young adults come home to Grady for the holiday, and by Wednesday night they need a break from their parents. The Moose has been the unofficial gathering spot since our parents were in their twenties. They even have a food truck or two parked outside so nobody needs to cook the night before a big meal. Benard's also gets a boost of business, but it's usually from the parents who also don't want to cook.

"It's another small-town tradition we're going to have to catch him up on, but I'm sure he'll come," I answer.

"Good . . . that little dweeb is growing on me."

Sixteen

"I LOVE THIS. I love everything about this," Nolan yells over the music with a slight slur from his second brandy old fashioned. "I feel like I could write a book about this."

"Calm down, Truman Capote, the townsfolk will revolt. The only reason they are accepting you as a podcaster is because I vouch for you, and they aren't really sure what a podcaster even is," I tell him, leaning forward to kiss his cheek. It is amazing how comfortable I've become with this man, who was a stranger just months ago.

Mal understandably decided to stay home and keep a still-healing Dougie company, and the aunts are running the restaurant so Nicole and I can enjoy our Wednesday before Thanksgiving tradition. Other than keeping one eye out for Chelsey to show up, the night feels refreshingly normal. I've introduced Nolan to dozens of people I went to high school with, and I'm surprised to say that he's found common ground with most of them. He just returned from a thirty-minute chat in the corner with Greg Connell about the future of A.I., which also surprises me because Greg is the same boy

95

who bribed me to take the ACTs for him and wouldn't talk to me for a month when I refused.

Nicole is in all her glory, acting as the life of the party to impress Karli. I can't even allow myself to be annoyed because I'm so relieved to see her smiling. To be honest, I'm equally as relieved to see Karli smiling after what she's been going through with her separation. They both deserve a little happiness today, and a few beers in a crowded dive bar is the perfect way to forget their troubles for a few hours.

Courtney, Nicole's still-in-the-closet and newly married former lover is here and looks absolutely heartsick that Nic is here with another woman. Normally this would make her night, but I'm not sure Nicole has even noticed she's here. She is focused almost entirely on Karli, which is a rarity for my best friend. I see her introduce Karli to a few of our old classmates, and I wonder what title she's giving to her new romantic interest. Too soon to call her a girlfriend, but anyone with two eyes can see she's more than a friend.

"What are you thinking?" Nolan asks me, watching my focused gaze on Nicole and Karli.

I smile and lean over the pub table to clasp my hand over his arm. "I'm just really happy that they seem to be having a good time. Lord knows they both deserve it."

He places his other hand on top of mine and squeezes.

"You deserve it just as much as anyone. You know that, right?"

I force my lips into a tight smile, but the truth is I don't feel I've done anything that warrants a break. Sure, I've had some not-so-great things happen in my life, but it's nothing compared to Nicole or my sister. Hell, even Dougie has had a rougher year than me. I just want to see the people I love catch a wave of better luck.

The lights from the parking lot shine into the dark bar as

the door is held open for a group of three guys I recognize from high school. I stiffen when I spot Mike Robinson, who works as a guard down at the jail. Nicole spots him at the same time and her entire mood changes. This is the man who most likely has kept watch over her dad since his arrest over a month ago. I know her enough to know she's partly embarrassed, but also curious as to what conditions her dad is enduring in the jail. She may hate the man, but she still loves him, if that makes any sense. I've picked my dad up enough times from his drunken shenanigans to know that even calling it a jail is generous. Most of the time I'd show up to bail him out and he'd have a cigarette hanging out of his mouth, playing Texas Hold 'Em with the guards on duty. I believe that's why we were all so quick to assume the attack on Lincoln Palmer was an inside job—Grady Jail has had very few instances of violence in its sixty-year run as the only jail in a forty-mile radius, and the investigation into his beating has been quite hush-hush.

Nicole makes a beeline for him, and Nolan quickly follows me as I jog over to interfere with whatever she's planning to say.

"Hey Mike! Good to see you!" I pull him in for a tight hug and whisper in his ear, "Don't say anything about Rich that's going to upset her, please."

"Got it," he whispers back, and I'm so thankful I could cry. "So good to see you, too!" he shouts as we separate. "You must be the new squeeze," he says, holding his hand out to Nolan and then turning to hug Nicole. "What's up Little Lowery?"

"You still a big dumb idiot?" she asks him, and his crater-sized dimples display the relief he feels that she didn't jump right in to ask about Rich. To be honest, I think I just exhaled for the first time since he walked in.

"You still hooking up with married girls?" he shoots back, and they both laugh. *Thank goodness.*

My relief is short-lived when Andrew, a squeaky little pest who graduated with us and went on to work at Palmer's Resort, joins the group and ruins everything.

"What's up guys? How's life? Oh shit, Robinson, aren't you guarding Nicole's dad? That's gotta be nuts. I bet you want to knock him the fuck out. No offense, Nicole."

I could strangle him myself.

"Nah, man. It's a small town, so I end up knowing most of the inmates. It's just part of the job, my dude."

Okay, I might hug him again even tighter. I need to buy this man a round.

"I heard about Dougie. I told everyone that chick was psycho, but nobody wanted to listen to me," Andrew says to me, taking a sip of his light beer and glancing around the room, oblivious to the fact that everyone wants to slap him. Of course, Nolan's investigator ears perk up.

"What made you think she was psycho?" he asks Andrew.

"If she didn't have her head up Lincoln Palmer's ass, she was in her cabin with all the curtains closed. Nobody knew what the fuck she was up to in there, but it could be eighty degrees out and she wouldn't even have the windows open. The only time I saw her outside was when she bird watching or whatever the hell she was up to."

Nolan and I shoot each other curious glances.

"Bird watching, like up in the trees?" I ask.

"Nah, usually across the lake. Toward Benard's actually. Maybe she was spying on you guys!" He laughs and takes another drink of beer.

This schmuck could not have less of a clue if he tried. Mike notices the look between Nolan and me and speaks up.

"I've been hearing a lot of talk around the station; I'm sure she'll be caught soon."

I'm not sure if he's just saying that to make me feel better, but I hope it's the truth. With all the technology we use these days, I'm sure it's a little harder to stay hidden than it used to be. She'll slip up, and when she does, my family will be here waiting.

Seventeen

AFTER WE ARE FINISHED with all the Thanksgiving-to-go pickup orders at Benard's, we close down the restaurant at 2:00 p.m., carrying on the tradition my grandparents started in 1979. Although staying open on holidays can be a profitable decision, they grew tired of missing all the special moments with family.

The locals can place an order by the Monday before Thanksgiving and they'll receive a few slices of turkey, mashed potatoes and gravy, green beans, sweet potatoes, a roll, and a slice of pumpkin pie for less than twenty bucks. It's become so popular, we started doing it for Christmas, as well, about ten years ago.

Brenda locks the door after the last reserved meal is picked up—Mr. Sampson from across the lake arrived at 1:58 p.m., just as he does every year—and pops a cheap bottle of champagne, which has also become tradition.

Nolan and Karli have gone home to spend the holiday with their families, so it's just the aunts, Dougie, Mal, Nicole, me, and a very reluctant Robbie, who only agreed to stay after Lou strongarmed him. We all know the relationship with his parents has been tense since his arrest, and he had been dreading spending the holiday with his judgmental extended family. So, he told them he was scheduled to work at our restaurant and didn't get any argument out of them.

Dad will show up later, but he has too much money on the Lions today to have to *strain to hear the broadcast over a bunch of yapping broads*—direct quote. He would also like me to set aside two slices of pie—I heard him whisper to Nicole that she's in charge of making sure I don't get stingy when choosing his slices.

We divide and conquer. It ends up taking the group only forty minutes to perform all the closing duties of the restaurant, push a few tables together, decorate them with cheap tablecloths and napkins from last year's after-holiday clearance at Hobby Lobby, and arrange the place settings for everyone. Just as I turn all the dining room TVs on so we don't miss kickoff, Lou shouts that the turkey is ready. Without need for delegation, each of us goes back to the kitchen to grab a dish to bring to the table. Unsurprisingly, Dougie grabs the rolls because they are the lightest. I see Nicole eyeing the back of his knees, and I read her mind. "Don't," I mouth to her, and she rolls her eyes like I just ruined the only fun in her life.

Other than Robbie, who remains oblivious most of the time, I think we've all been keeping ourselves busy for the last few hours so we wouldn't be struck with the gravity of our first holiday with Mal in two decades. It's nearly too heavy to grasp; we've been sitting at this table for twenty years with an empty spot set for her. Twenty Thanksgivings staring out at that lake and wondering if her body was at the bottom of it. Now she's here, placing a dish full of Deb's famous sweet potato casserole at the center of the table, like she never left at all. Does she understand the ache we've felt for her, every moment that she was gone? Did she feel the same for us, or was there a year she finally gave up? The pit in my stomach grows when I remember the handful of times Rich and Mae joined us for Benard family Thanksgiving. They sat here and ate a homecooked meal made by my family, while they kept a missing member of ours in their basement. I've read plenty of books about psychopaths, but having a few in your own backyard makes you understand that these people really do exist. Not everyone in this world is inherently good.

Once we've all passed the serving dishes around the table and filled our plates, the room grows silent. We are no longer a church-affiliated family; that ended years ago. I'm not sure where the rest of my family stands on their beliefs, but rather than say grace, Brenda usually just gives a quick speech about how happy she is to have us all around the table. We all look to her to make her sentimental speech, but when her eyes land on Dougie and Malorie, both present, safe, and healthy, she loses it.

That's when it hits the rest of us. We're all here. Of course, we wish Mom was still alive and that Dad didn't have a gambling addiction, but this is the most complete holiday meal we've had in a very, very long time.

Tears are streaming down all our faces, even Robbie, God bless him.

"Would it be okay if I give the speech this year?" Malorie asks. Each one of us shouts some version of "Of course!" which makes us all laugh. Just as we are blotting our wet faces with the crispy napkins, which have cartoon turkeys printed on them, Mal stands with a half-full glass of champagne in her hand.

"I can't begin to imagine what you guys went through while I was gone. Except for you, Robbie," she begins, and this gets a laugh from everyone in the room. "While I sat in that room and ached for my family, you all had to sit here not knowing if I was alive or dead. I wouldn't wish that on anyone."

Nicole hangs her head when Mal mentions *that room* and I think she'll continue to do that for years until she accepts the fact that we forgive her and would never hold her accountable for the actions of her family.

"I kept wishing for just one more Thanksgiving or just one more Christmas; hell, I got so desperate, I even wished for one more shift with Dougie, where we both got put on bathroom duty because of our smart mouths," she says, holding her glass in Dougie's direction, and he returns the gesture with a sly grin. "I know the time since I've been back has been filled with so much chaos—they'll surely come film an episode of Dateline here that will be too wild to believe—but the important thing is I'm home. Dougie is home. Nicole, you are part of our family. Hell, Robbie is welcome to be part of the family, too. The final puzzle pieces will be finding Dennis and Chelsey so they can be locked up for their sick crimes, and then we can try our best to live a normal life. So, thank you all for holding out hope that I would come home, and cheers to a happy and uneventful life for all of us going forward. I'm so damn happy to be back with you all on my favorite eating holiday."

Everyone stands to clink glasses, and there isn't a dry eye in the room.

"I just want to make a quick announcement as well," Lou says, coughing to disguise the emotion in her voice as she often does. "We all know I'm not ready to let Mal completely out of my sight just yet . . . but cut me a break; she's barely been home a month, you know? Anyways, Brenda, Deb, and I have been talking, and we're building an extra cabin on the empty lot next to number eight. Katie and Mal, we'd like you to live there for as long as you'd like. We've got the floor plans made for a two bedroom, two bath, and we think it would be just perfect for you girls. It will give you a little freedom while also keeping you close enough so I can sleep at night. Your dad cleared the land this morning and will be ready to break ground on construction in the next day or two."

Despite both of us pushing the age of forty, we celebrate like we are two broke college kids who were just handed the keys to freedom. I cannot think of a better gift. Mal hugs my neck before pulling back to look into my eyes and confirm that this is what I truly want.

"Thank goodness! I was getting sick of sharing a bathroom with you again. You get toothpaste everywhere," I tell her with a wink.

"What about me?" Dougie asks, clearly offended by the slight.

"You'll be fine," Lou says in her signature gruff tone.

"Oh, Lou, tell him," Brenda pleads.

Lou rolls her eyes before adding, "The clearing on the opposite end, next to cabin one, has your name on it. Once the snow clears, we'll get yours started."

Dougie raises his hands over his head in celebration. You'd think we were all helpless kids, rather than able-bodied adults who shouldn't need their family to provide their housing.

One by one, we all begin to eat our dinner and talk about the off season, listing all the projects we need to complete around the property before the tourists arrive in May. Robbie seems quite relieved that we'll have more than enough work to keep him employed over the winter. I plan to ask Lou tonight if we should let him stay in one of the guest cabins for the next few months until he gets things sorted out with his family. They are rarely at capacity, and I'm sure she'd love to have an on-call employee so close when she needs him.

"Wait," I say, getting everyone's attention. "I can't believe we let our guard down. There's a catch; there's always a catch. What is it?"

Deb, also known as the world's worst liar, coughs into her

napkin. That's one of her tells. Brenda shoots a look in Lou's direction that pleads for her to be the one to break it to us.

"Well, kids, you know we aren't getting any younger. The truth is, we'd all like to at least have retirement somewhere in our sights. If we have the three of you here to take over, we think it would be a great way to back away from the business and keep the tradition of Benard's being a family-run resort."

Nolan is the first thing that pops in my mind, which is a foreign feeling. I never focus too much on a future with anyone; I didn't even allow myself to do it much when I was engaged to Dave. Would Nolan want to live in Grady? If we end up together, could he operate his podcast from the lake? Although I've only known him for months, I can absolutely picture him making that sacrifice for me, and the funny part is, I don't even think it would be that much of a sacrifice. This place is really growing on him.

Dougie and Mal seem to be contemplating the offer as well. None of us are completely opposed to it, but we aren't enthusiastically committing, either.

"I could see the three of us taking over the business," Mal says to my surprise, "but on one condition—we all take vacation time. I love you three, and this is no slight to you, but I don't want to work myself to death and never take time off. I want to see the world. If we can find a happy medium with us keeping the business afloat while also prioritizing our personal lives, I think we could probably make it work."

Without words, I know we're all on the same page. The three of us are going to be the future of Benard's Lakeside Inn, and if I'm lucky enough, Nolan will be by my side when we get the keys.

Eighteen

IT NEVER FEELS good to receive a gift when it comes at the expense of someone else's well-being, so none of us have admitted out loud how relieved we are that two separate national tragedies have taken the attention away from the Benard family this week. A mass shooting in Buffalo and a late-in-the-season category five hurricane approaching the coast of Florida have caused the news media to all but forget we exist. It's the perfect day for Malorie to experience life as a normal human—with an eight-hour shift at work.

While the rest of us are guzzling coffee and dragging our feet, my sister is whistling an off-key version of a cartoon theme song while she dices potatoes and labels food containers for the walk-in cooler. I keep catching her gazing out the window over the prep sink and smiling. You can't even see the lake from that window; it's just a view of the wooded path leading to one of the guest cabins, but she shakes her head every time she catches a glimpse, like she can't believe how lucky she is to be staring at a bunch of trees.

Dad and his crew arrived early this morning to continue

construction on our "Sister Cabin," as we've begun calling it, and he even caved into our demands for a patio facing the lake. The thought of having a steaming cup of coffee with my sister in our matching lounge chairs while we wave to the fishermen as they glide by is the perfect, quiet life of my dreams.

Speaking of the life of my dreams, Nolan is coming back to town today after a week in Wisconsin with his parents. He's going to conduct a few interviews for the final episode of this season before going on a five-city press tour to promote the podcast. He said he's taking a break for the Christmas season when he's done, but I haven't had the courage to ask him where that break will be spent. Dad says our cabin should be done by Christmas, and when Lou questioned that timeline, Dad responded, "Lady, if I tell you a rooster can tow a freight train, don't ask questions—just hitch him up," to which Lou acted annoyed, but I could tell she was trying hard not to smile.

The restaurant hasn't been any busier than normal, but the tips have been fantastic. I'm not sure if the locals are pleased that the press has left town or if everyone's just happy with the mild start to winter, but I've been making a minimum of twenty percent across the board. Curtis Rivers even stopped in with his wife and their son, Brogan, and they left a twenty-dollar bill, which is more than he's ever left me or any other server at Benard's in the decades he's been coming here.

I've been saving my tips to surprise Mal with a fancy coffee maker for our new cabin. I took her to Escanaba yesterday to run errands, and after driving through Bigby Coffee for a caramel latte, she has a newfound obsession for crafted coffee drinks. We went to town early enough in the morning that she was able to walk through the grocery store undetected. Although, the cashier seemed to do a double take as we were paying for our order, nobody said a word to her. I don't want to put words in her mouth, but I feel like this has been the first week that she is able to picture herself having a normal life. I'm sure she has been questioning whether that would be possible with strangers camped outside our lodge and restaurant day and night.

Right before the lunch rush at Benard's, our hostess tells me that she sat me with a one-top and gives me an apologetic look, which means it's either a cranky local I'm familiar with, or an equally difficult out-of-towner.

I exit the kitchen to perform my usual greeting and see it's a woman around my age with an expensive suit, laptop, and an iPhone glued to her ear. My first instinct is to assume she's a journalist, but as I get closer, I see the logo for the State of Michigan's website open on her MacBook. I recognize it because the PR firm I worked for in Lansing helped design it.

She places her hand over the mouthpiece of her phone and mouths *Diet Coke* to me, and when I come back to bring her drink and take her order, she simply points to the Autumn Harvest Salad on the menu and gives me a thumbs up before going back to her conversation. With my back to her, I ring her order in on the point-of-sale screen and can't help but overhear a little of her discussion. This woman is *stressed*. She's on her way to Marquette from Grand Rapids; I'm not sure how she found us, but we're included on countless worth-the-drive lists for small town supper clubs, so it's not all that unheard of for tourists to make the detour on their way to a bigger town.

It would be dramatic to say that I have PTSD from my years as a career woman, but as I hear the familiar phrases she's using to appease whoever is on the other end of the phone, my heartbeat races and a small, throbbing knot forms in my stomach. I have long known how good it feels to be home, but it's in this exact moment that I realize I *never* want to go back to that life.

Long hours at the office, even longer hours at home handling after-hours crises that could have waited until morning, and boss-babe superiors who think being overworked is a badge of honor—it's all nonsense. Here, by the lake, serving cocktails and watching the sunset each night—it's where I belong.

The woman pays with a business American Express card, leaves exactly eighteen percent, and exits the restaurant without actually speaking a word to me. Luckily, her icy demeanor is balanced out by the next guests to sit at her table —the Grady Lake Women's Knitting Club. In case there was any confusion, they are all wearing matching crewneck sweatshirts with the group's name emblazoned in a goofy font that resembles a string of yarn.

Despite fawning over me and reminding me how lovely I am, and how I'm looking more like my mother every day, their moods quickly change when Nicole walks in, and I am tickled over their long-held grudge with her.

"Hello, ladies. I'm sure you're happy that Katie has moved home so we won't be missing anymore Labor Day boat parades," she says to them before tipping her baseball cap and taking a seat at the bar with her backs to them.

Every year that I've come home to enter the contest with Nicole, we've edged out the knitting club to take the trophy. They spend weeks on their "boat float" and have won first prize each year we don't enter. Although I'm on the team with Nicole and Dougie, they seem to single out Nicole as their nemesis and have gone as far as accusing her of cheating. *This* is the small-town drama I've been missing. I don't want kidnapping, assaults, murder—I want a group of elderly women who despise my best friend for besting them in a holiday boat parade.

I smile as they roll their eyes at Nicole in unison as she orders a Bloody Mary from Dougie.

"You know, she's actually been wanting to learn how to knit," I lie, gesturing back to Nicole.

"Really?" asks Edith, the ringleader of the group. "Well, we have a pretty flexible schedule this winter. I guess we could show the poor thing the basics."

Her tight-lipped smirk nearly sends me over the edge.

"I'll let her know; she'll be thrilled to learn such a valuable new skill from a talented group of ladies like you," I say while leaning forward to refill each of their coffee mugs.

"You are just an absolute gem. I bet your father is so proud of you," says Alice while she adds a third packet of sugar to her coffee. "Oh, speak of the handsome devil."

I turn to see Dad walking in the side door, his boots covered in mud, plaster, and God knows what else.

"Ladies, how is it possible you all look half your age? Is it something in the water?" he asks with his signature Charles David smile.

"Oh, Chuck, you're too much!" shouts Edith with mock outrage.

Dad kisses each of their hands before taking his seat at the bar next to Nicole. You'd think Elvis Presley himself just arrived in Grady with how these ladies are reacting. I'm going to have to refill all their ice waters before they overheat.

"Still got it," Nicole whispers to Dad before fist-bumping him.

"What you've *still got* is the ability to piss Lou off when she sees all that dirt you just tracked in with your work boots," I tell him.

"That woman can't scare me," he says, and with the comedic timing of a '90s sitcom, Lou comes out of the kitchen, spots the mud, and her eyes travel directly to Dad. There may well be actual steam coming from her ears as she stomps over to him.

"Chuck," she says through gritted teeth.

"Yes, my darling ex-sister-in-law, of course I'll be grabbing the broom to sweep this up before I leave. You know, to go build the cabin on your property for the cost of materials, no labor charges included," Dad says before taking a sip of his iced tea. Thank goodness it's not vodka.

"The day Chuck David does something that doesn't make him a little profit is the day I quit my job and become a nun at St. Joseph's. I wasn't born yesterday," Lou grumbles before batting a dismissive hand at him and turning to me. "Table thirty-two's food is up, sweetheart."

"Sweetheart? Why can't you talk to me like that?" Dad asks with a shit-eating grin.

"Because you're a pain in my ass, Chuck. Now order your lunch and get back to work."

When I enter the kitchen, Robbie and Mal are working the expo station together. He's showing her how to garnish plates, and she's telling him how we used to do it *back in her day*.

"Did you even have computers to ring in orders back then?" he asks, without a hint of playfulness in his voice, just genuine curiosity.

"No, we just hand wrote everything down on these little green guest checks and hung them up here in the window. Lou was usually running expo, and she'd just shout the orders back to the kitchen," Mal explains.

"Whoa," Robbie replies, looking up at the top of the kitchen line to visualize where we used to stick the guests checks. I remember Friday nights fondly; it was controlled chaos. We'd get a good butt kicking each weekend, but it was so fun to sit around and tell our war stories after the shift. Sitting on the back patio with Mal as we untied our dirty aprons and counted our tips is one of those memories I didn't realize was so special until I was old enough to reflect.

"Don't act so shocked, you little shit. I'm not that old," Malorie tells him with a light punch on the arm.

"You're decently old," I declare, reaching forward to grab the plates for my table. I don't have to wait around to know she's scoffing at me. I'm so damn happy to have her back.

When I push the kitchen exit door open with my hip, I see Dad and Lou alone at the bar. Nicole has left, most likely to help at the Grab N Go. Much like us, she cuts down her staff levels in the off season and does a lot of work herself. Now that the out-of-towners have gone home, it's relatively safe for her to work the counter and not get hounded by journalists or nosey internet sleuths. Nobody has brought up the fact that the business probably needs to get put in her name now that Grandma Mae is gone and Rich is in jail, and I'm going to give it a little more time before I do. There's also the matter of what is going to happen to Rich's cabin and the vacant lot that held the bunkers, but that is *definitely* a conversation for another day.

I deliver the food to my table, cash out the knitting club, and return to the bar to catch my breath and see what Lou and Dad are talking about. As soon as I finish pouring myself a Sprite with the bar gun and getting cussed out by Dougie for being behind the bar while I'm clocked in as a server, a familiar face walks through the front door of the restaurant. Ken Barron, a local attorney who happens to be the unfortunate sleazeball that agreed to represent Rich Lowery.

"What do you call ten thousand lawyers at the bottom of the ocean?" Dad shouts to him in place of a normal greeting.

"Yeah, yeah, *a good start*. I heard that joke the first day of law school," Ken replies before joining them at the bar and giving Dougie and me a pleasant hello.

"What do lawyers use for birth control?" Lou chimes in.

"Their personalities," Ken answers with a shake of the

head. "I never understood that one; I think we have great personalities."

"You would," Lou replies under her breath.

"To what do we owe the pleasure of a visit from the scumbag representing the monster who held my daughter captive in his basement for half her life?" Dad asks a little more lightheartedly than I would have expected. If Rich's lawyer was anyone other than the man who grew up across the alley from Dad, Ken would be taking a real beating, and it might not just be verbal.

"I wanted to come tell the family in person that there won't be a trial. Rich has decided to plead guilty to all charges, including withholding evidence—the tapes that were found on his property. He's also given the police the location of one more camera that was still active and rolling at the time of his arrest, which he doesn't believe the search teams discovered. Sheriff Nelson and his boys are on the property now to retrieve it."

"So, what's the catch?" Lou asks. "I mean, I'm thankful Mal isn't going to have to testify, but I know there's a catch."

"He would like the judge to sign a deal that makes him eligible for parole in twenty years," Ken answers.

Dad huffs loudly and spins a few degrees in his barstool before Lou holds up a hand in his direction.

"So there'd be no possible chance of parole before the twenty years are up?" she asks.

"No ma'am."

"Give him the deal. That spares this family from a drawn-out trial and that son of a bitch will be in his eighties before he sees the light of day again. The minute he steps out of that prison, I'll make him wish he'd chosen a life sentence," Lou says without a hint of humor.

"Now Lou, you know you can't threaten my client in front of me," Ken warns her.

"It's not a threat," she replies without breaking eye contact.

"What about the baby?" I ask. "Can we make it part of the deal that he has to tell us where he buried Mal's baby?"

Ken puts both hands in the pockets of his expensive suit and shrugs. "I'll give it another try, but so far, he's not budging. The only thing he'd tell me is that it's better for everyone if Malorie doesn't know what happened to that child."

Nineteen

TODAY IS one of those mornings where you want time to slow down. Maybe if I don't make any sudden movements, we can stay a little longer in this dreamlike state without anyone coming to our door with bad news.

This doesn't just apply to someone like me, who is a part of a family that has received an abnormal amount of bad news. Think of a normal human with a normal amount of tragedy in their normal lives—if they are having a morning like mine, no matter how idyllic it is, they will inevitably be snapped out of it by an unexpected call from their demanding boss, a cut to their finger while dicing vegetables that's much deeper than they initially thought, a car that backs into their vehicle in the grocery store parking lot and drives away. *Something* inconvenient or bad happens to everyone. Nobody can live in a state of bliss forever. That's why I'm taking in every second of my lazy morning with Mal and not dwelling on the fact that sooner rather than later, it will end.

Against all odds, we were both able to sleep in today. Not even heavy-footed Dougie woke us from our early winter slumber. Deb had a doctor's appointment in Marquette, so she's making a day of it and doing a little shopping while Lou, Brenda, and Dougie run the restaurant. Nicole is busy at the Grab N Go, and Dad is trying to get some framing done on the cabin with his crew before the storm arrives. So, it's just Mal and me at the lodge.

Grady Lake isn't that large, but it's still quite an ominous sight when the storm clouds roll in over the water. The temperature is right on the cusp of being cold enough for snow, but it's most likely going to start as rain. By nightfall, the roads will be slick as hell, so I hope Nolan arrives in Grady soon.

We are both on our second cups of coffee, in our respective lounge chairs in front of the patio windows in the family room. The *Today* show is on TV, but neither of us are really paying attention because we are too focused on watching the gray clouds forming across the lake. I know it's just an optical illusion, but I would swear they are hanging directly above Palmer's abandoned resort. Who knows what the hell is going to happen to that place; it's a multi-million-dollar eyesore in my opinion, but it would be a shame to have such a large portion of our lake sit vacant. I'm not sure what typically happens in these situations, but I'm assuming the bank will auction it off to the highest bidder. I cringe thinking about another out-of-town family buying up such valuable real estate in Grady, but let's be honest—could they be any worse than the Palmers?

"I promise I'm not saying this to get any sympathy, but this feels like an absolute luxury. The days that I almost lost hope, this is the kind of morning that kept me going. The thought that I could be having coffee with my little sister, with nothing on my agenda but waiting for November winds to wreak havoc on us."

I take my focus off the clouds for a moment to look at my sister.

"Mal, you deserve sympathy from everyone you meet for the rest of your life. You literally have not gotten to watch a storm rolling in for two decades. I'll sit here with you all day if you want," I tell her.

"Don't use me as an excuse to sit on your ass all day," she says, scrunching her nose. I smile because I'm starting to see the youthful glow reappear. She looked so tired, sick, and defeated the day she came home. Now she looks like my sister, and that was something I worried I'd never be able to say again.

Lou talked Nelson into backing down on the armed guards, and they compromised—two of Grady's finest are parked outside in their patrol car, watching anyone who comes in or out of the lodge. Today it's two guys I went to school with, Jonas and Corey, and I'm assuming they both have a face full of Grab N Go donuts because Nolan walks right by their car without question, and within seconds I hear him jogging up the back stairs.

"As long as you're getting up, want to get me another cup?" Mal asks, holding her empty mug in my direction. It's a First Bank mug, and I think it's been in this lodge since Mom was around.

I get to the door right as Nolan knocks, and I scare the daylights out of him when I swing it open and see his raised fist and wide-eyed stare. He laughs and lowers his hand to his heart, which makes me smile because damn, his laugh is perfect.

"I was just standing here waiting for you," I say with a wink. "My legs were starting to get sore."

I set Mal's mug down on the counter and turn back around to hug him. He has a large manila envelope in one hand, and it crinkles against my back when he returns the hug.

"What's this?" I ask.

"Is it just you two here?" he asks without answering my

question. He waves a quick hello to Mal, and I wonder if it's still strange for him to be looking at the subject of a missing persons case that haunted him for years. It must be even stranger to be dating her sister.

"Don't tell me you're on the list of people afraid to come over when Lou is here," Mal shouts from the family room.

"No, it's not that. Well, yes, technically I'm terrified of her, but I was asking because I'm hoping to talk to you both alone," Nolan replies.

He declines my offer of coffee, so I top Mal's off, and we all convene in the family room. Mal and I in our chairs and Nolan on the loveseat closest to me. He's fidgeting with the envelope, and his usual nervous tick has started—he's tapping his leg at an abnormally fast rate.

"Nolan, whatever it is, my sister and I can handle it," Mal says, reaching over to place her hand on mine.

"She's right, whatever it is—we've heard worse."

"Well, I'm happy to say, I might be the first person to show up unannounced with *good* news at this lodge."

This stirs something in me. Nolan knows me. He knows my family. He knows what we've been through; hell, what we continue to go through. Making a joke about how much bad news we usually get at this lodge just made it hit me all at once that Nolan could be part of this family. I try to swallow the lump in my throat so I don't get so emotional over something so silly.

"I have a spot on our website where listeners can pay for a monthly subscription that gets them bonus content, a t-shirt, a bunch of extras. I never pay too much attention to it because Karli handles it, and it's basically just extra money we use to travel for work. Well, once this season hit number one on the charts, she added a button where listeners could click to donate money to help Malorie reacclimate and maybe do a little traveling that she's missed out on. Karli said she didn't mention it to me because she figured it would be a couple hundred dollars and she'd just cut a check to give you guys on Christmas."

Malorie and I look at each other . . . I grasp that he's about to tell us the check is going to be more than he expected, but this is a lot of information to take in. Malorie simply looks confused. Nolan opens the envelope and pulls out a few sheets of white paper and what appears to be a check.

"This is a ledger of everyone who donated, although some chose to remain anonymous. Karli closed out the account this week and had a check cut for you. Here you go, Mal. I hope you get to see every place you've ever dreamed of," Nolan says, and his hand is shaking as he hands it all over to my sister. I make eye contact with him while she is unfolding the check and small pools are forming at the bottom of his eyes, threatening to spill over. This man genuinely loves me, doesn't he? He wants good things for my sister so badly, he's an emotional wreck over giving her this news. Maybe it will be a couple grand, and she and I can make that trip to Key West we always talked about.

"This can't be right," she says, staring at the check. "There's no way. Someone must have clicked the wrong button or something . . . right?"

"No, Malorie, it's right. The average donation was twenty dollars; we just had a lot of people donate. A lot of people who are happy you're home and want good things for you," he says, and the way he is genuinely smiling at her good fortune makes something deep in my body hum.

"Well, are you going to tell me?" I ask, clapping my hands together in anticipation.

"Katie . . . this check is written out for over two hundred thousand dollars. This is going to change our lives."

Twenty

"NOW, this might change the circumstances of my hourly rate," Dad says with a shrug before leaning forward to serve himself another slice of pizza.

"Like hell it will, Chuck. Shut up and drink your cheap beer. We're celebrating," Lou barks. She holds up her own glass, a rare serving of wine for my oldest aunt, and proposes a toast. "To Nolan and Karli, the only two journalists on this planet who I don't want to strangle. You two stuck your necks out for our family, and now you've changed Malorie's life once more with your kindness."

We all raise our glasses in their honor as shouts of *Cheers* and *Hear, Hear* ring out around the table. We're in the back room at Johnny's, which barely fits our group, causing the server to squeeze her way around the table each time we need another refill. She doesn't seem to mind because she knows the family and knows how we tip. The Benards, Nicole, Dad, Nolan, Karli—we're all here. The blissful morning I didn't want to end has somehow transformed into an even better night.

Just as the group quiets after Lou's toast, a pang of

thunder rings out so loud, I swear I feel the floors vibrate. This is odd for the week before December, but the unusual storm also brought with it an air of excitement. Pizza and beer with all the people I love and the comfort of knowing that my sister isn't going to have to worry about money for a long time— what could be better?

It was a stark reminder of how long she'd been gone when we discussed picking out a vehicle for her and she asked if there was a new model of Grand Am she could look at. Dad blew out a long and hard breath before breaking the bad news to her about Pontiac's demise.

Other than my surprise birthday party at The Moose Trap, which was for friends and family only, this is Mal's first time having dinner in public. I keep glancing over in her direction to make sure she seems comfortable, but I don't want to focus on her too much because she'll notice and get annoyed with me. "I'm supposed to be the big sister," she continues to tell me each time I make a fuss over her well-being.

Rich's lawyer had a meeting with Nicole separately to discuss Rich's intentions to change his plea to guilty and make a deal with prosecutors for twenty years and then possible parole. There's no guarantee it's going to be accepted, but with the blessing of our family, I can't see why it won't be. It's saving everyone a lot of time and money if this case doesn't go to trial. We want Rich to pay for what he did as much as anyone, but putting Malorie on the stand and reigniting a media firestorm isn't in anyone's best interest. When I asked Nicole what she thought of the situation, she seemed very disinterested in discussing her dad and just replied, "I'm just ready for it to be over with," and shrugged.

Dougie hasn't talked much about his dad, but he rarely did even before he was wanted for kidnapping and assault charges. It's a hard case because prosecutors haven't identified the girl on the video with Dennis, and no further victims have come forward. Lincoln is dead, so they don't even have proof of what went on in the bunker. It's not the news we wanted to hear, but the visiting detectives have been very clear that finding him may drop down on the priority list if they can't find any additional evidence of his crimes. They did interview Rich Lowery about it and he confirmed that he knew Dennis well and signed an affidavit stating that he was only on the trail cam footage the first year or so after the bunkers were dug. Rich described feeling relieved that his friend came to his senses and quit working with Lincoln Palmer. Any suggestion that Rich himself was involved with Palmer was quickly squashed after the first few interviews in jail, where he spewed so many curse words when asked about Lincoln, they had to stop the tape from recording several times and remind him to watch his temper.

Our server brings out the check and announces that Johnny's is closing a little early because the downpour of rain is slowly turning to sleet, and the local TV station is predicting the roads are going to be a "real shitshow in an hour or two," but I'm sure the meteorologist chose less colorful words.

"Eh, might as well close the restaurant down a little early, too. You know, to stay on the safe side," Lou declares, and we all smile because we know she's been on edge all night thinking about the employees running the place without any of us there. "I'll stop by and let them know."

Nolan leans close and whispers in my ear, "Want to have a sleepover? I've missed you." My body says yes with a throbbing pulse before the decision even reaches my brain. He was only gone a week and I feel like part of me has been missing. I jump when I see motion from the corner of my eye, just inches away, behind my chair.

It's Nicole, squatted down with her face directly in the middle of Nolan and me.

"Can I come, too?" she asks with a devious grin before

tipping her nearly empty Coors Light bottle back to retrieve the last few drops.

"I'm sure Karli would be happy to have a sleepover with you," I answer in a mildly sarcastic tone.

"Wow, so you're saying your sleepover would be more fun without me? Rude." She sets her empty bottle on the table between us and rubs her knuckles on my scalp before going back over to Karli.

As we are all standing and putting on our light winter coats, I catch the sight of Dougie shamelessly flirting with our server. The man was nearly killed by his last romantic interest; you'd think he'd take a little breather from the ladies. I shake my head in disbelief as he details how he "fought for his life" and is currently "helping the detectives find that crazy bitch." Maybe he should throw in a story about saving a baby from a burning building to really close the deal. Against all odds, she appears to be hanging on his every word.

Luckily, we are close enough to the resort that the pure sleet falling sideways from the darkened skies isn't much of an issue until it's time to get back out of our vehicles. Nolan and I run for his cabin. I decide that I can sleep in one of his shirts because going to the lodge and back to his cabin would result in getting even more soaked than I already am. Just as we get to the front door, an intense burst of lightning fills the sky, giving the entire lake a fireworks show.

"Thunder sleet?" he asks as we get inside and lock the door behind us.

"I wish I could tell you it's a normal occurrence, but this may be a first."

He takes a few steps across the small cabin to grab us each a large bath towel, throwing his over his right shoulder before wrapping mine around my body and kissing my forehead. We stand like that for a minute and just breathe. The thunder continues to boom through the night sky every minute or so, and the sleet is so heavy the sounds of it slapping the windows echo through the quiet cabin. Without moving from the entryway, he kisses me, and I melt right into him. I've missed him this week . . . He's the first thing I think about in the morning and the last thing at night. I'm not sure why I've been fighting it so hard, but I love this man. This isn't a crush, it isn't a fascination with a man who helped save my sister, and it's not just situational. I'm certain the feelings I have for Nolan won't disappear when life begins to get back to normal. I want him to move here. I want my life to include him every day.

I can't think of a better night for it to finally happen, and it does. Slow at first and passionate at the end; Nolan feels better than I could have ever imagined. The night sky illuminates the cabin walls from the explosions of lightning, giving me glimpses of his smooth, olive skin. I run my hands through his hair, and he enjoys it, rather than pushing me away like Dave used to. Best of all, when we are done, I feel nothing but love. He is attentive, caring, and his top priority is ensuring that I'm comfortable. He momentarily panics when a tear slides down my right cheek, but I tell him it's a happy tear. It's my body showing relief from feeling like I'm right where I belong for the first time in a long, long while.

Twenty-One

"I TALKED to Nicole and she's going to join me for my session with Dalia today," Mal mentions casually as she pours herself a bowl of cereal. Nicole has avoided therapy for as long as I've known her, but I also know she'll do anything to regain my sister's trust, so I guess it's not all that surprising.

"I think that's great," I tell her in all sincerity. "I know it's a big ask, but forgiving her would lift a huge weight off her shoulders. I can see it in her eyes every time you're around."

She retrieves milk from the fridge to top off her cereal with a side of sliced bananas, just as she did in high school. I wonder how many mornings underground she longed for this simple routine.

"I can, too. The thing is, I believe her, Katie. I believed her the second she explained herself about the medication she was on. Unfortunately, I've taken similar meds against my will, and I know how it can fuck with your memory and sense of reality. I guess I just needed someone to be mad at, so I stayed mad a little longer than I should have."

"No Mal, you had every right to be mad. When I overheard you two in our room, I almost lost it on her. I'm just glad we both gave her the opportunity to explain. We're the only family she has left, and I'm not sure I could have stomached having to cut her out of our lives, but I would have if she didn't have a valid explanation."

My phone lights up on the counter and I'm surprised to see Sheriff Nelson's number on the screen. It's nine in the morning. I hold it up to show Mal who's calling before I answer. She furrows her brows and motions for me to hurry and take the call.

"Hi Sheriff! You're working bright and early, I see," I singsong, not sure why I am feeling the need to be so phony with him this morning.

"Katie, I'm glad you answered. Any chance you have a minute to stop by the station this morning, or are you working a shift?" he asks.

"That depends, am I being arrested?" I joke. He barks out a short, uncomfortable laugh.

"Of course not, I just want to go over some evidence that was just handed over to me by the boys in blue," he says, referring to the Michigan State Police, who have all but taken over his investigations. He's been treated like an outsider since his suspension.

"On which case?" I ask, still in disbelief that there is more than one case he could be referencing.

"Chelsey Benoit," he responds with no further details.

"Okay, give me ten minutes to get dressed and freshen up, and I'll be right over."

Mal, ever the helpful sister, already has a Styrofoam cup and lid down from the cabinet for my coffee after hearing my end of the conversation. "What do you think is going on?" she asks, crunching on her cereal.

"I'm not sure, but it's strange he's just calling me instead of me and Lou. I'll head down there, but if you see the aunts, please let them know where I'm at," I tell her, turning toward our bedroom. "You'll be okay here for a little while?"

She smiles. "We've still got Tweedle-Dee and Tweedle-Dum outside in their patrol car; who would dream of messing with me?"

* * *

"I apologize for the delay. Ever since an inmate was attacked in my jail and my name showed up on Rich's tapes that were logged in evidence, I've apparently been moved down on the chain of command in my own county. My name was cleared over a week ago, and I'm still being handed evidence after everyone and their mother has viewed it," Nelson tells me as I take a seat across from him in his office. It's nice being in this spacious, bright area for a change. I was getting quite tired of the small, stuffy investigation rooms my family usually gets ushered into.

I raise my eyebrow as to say "anything else you want to get off your chest before you tell me why I'm here?" but I keep my mouth shut because I'm not trying to annoy him before he can give me whatever dirt he's discovered on Chelsey.

"As part of Rich Lowery's plea agreement, he has identified the location of two additional cameras on his acreage which were not discovered by the search team. It looks like there is nearly a month of recordings on each device, which have been viewed by the detectives. Some of it is a little difficult to watch, so I'm going to sum it up for you. I think after watching the footage, we can attribute at least two additional homicides to Chelsey Benoit."

"Two?" I gasp.

"It appears she gave the final blow to Mrs. Fallon Palmer, formerly Ashley Smith, as she saved Sammie Spencer and tried to get away from Chelsey and Lincoln. We have footage weeks later of Sammie taking photos of the lake while it was snowing and, although she walks off camera toward the North Cove, we see Chelsey Benoit following closely behind her."

I *knew* Sammie Spencer's death wasn't accidental. Yes, I understand how dangerous that thicket under the surface of the cove can be, but I couldn't picture her getting close enough to the water that she'd fall in. Especially in the cold weather, it just didn't make sense. I wanted to believe the sheriff when he said it was clearly an accidental drowning, but something just nagged in the back of my brain that screamed ASK MORE QUESTIONS, but so much else was going on in our lives, I put it on the back burner. I cannot imagine the outrage her mother is going to feel when she gets the news, if she hasn't received it already.

"This is obviously pretty shocking news, but I'm not sure why it was me specifically you chose to tell it to? Why wouldn't you call Lou?" I ask.

Nelson reaches behind him to retrieve a file folder and opens it, pulling out a few sheets and laying them out across his solid oak desk. They are black and white stills that appear to be taken from a security camera. I'm not close enough to make out who is in the pictures.

"When we learned that Chelsey was married to your ex-fiancé, we paid him a visit and did some digging. Little bit of a smug fella; glad you got rid of that one," he says, taking his eyes off the photos to give me a look much like my father would. "He gave us your name, of course, as well as two other individuals he carried on relations with while he was married to Chelsey."

I scoff. I knew of one—Bagel Girl—but wasn't aware of any other scandalous affairs. You'd think it would hurt me to hear this, but mentally I am in another world now, not the one I lived in with Dave. The months we've been separated feel like years.

"Jackie Logan and Alison Simpson," he announces, followed by a pause for my reaction. Against my best efforts at nonchalance, I flinch. Jackie was the worker at the bagel shop down the street, who I already knew about, but Alison . . . Alison was my coworker at the PR agency. She was my confidante. We even went to Chicago on a girl's weekend together. *You're telling me she was sleeping with my fiancé?*

"I was aware of Jackie. I know Alison, but I didn't realize she was carrying on a relationship with my fiancé."

"I'm sorry you had to find out like this," Nelson says, and I believe him.

"It's okay, Sheriff. I'm finding out that Dave wasn't at all the man I believed him to be, so I guess it's not all that surprising. Well, other than the fact that it was with Alison. I didn't see that coming."

"The reason these two particular women are so important to the case is that they both had close family members suffer random tragedies in the last year. Chelsey Benoit is an official suspect in both cases."

"What?" I ask, I'm entirely too shocked and confused to grasp what this means. "Are you saying she was methodically hurting people to punish the women Dave was sleeping with? How would she even know about Alison and Jackie? I only knew about one of them and I lived with the man. What kind of tragedies?"

Nelson pulls out a typed report from the file. "It looks like Jackie's only brother was critically injured in a hit-and-run accident while jogging, and Alison's mother was attacked by a new student who signed up to take piano lessons at her house under a fake name. Luckily, street cameras from the accident and a doorbell camera at the Simpson residence both show a suspect who fits the description of Chelsey Benoit."

My stomach drops. *Dougie.* She hurt Dougie to punish me.

"We're interviewing all the former employees of Palmer's Resort that we can find, and so far, we've gotten some pretty disturbing information. I don't have enough evidence to prove it quite yet, but I think Chelsey found out about Lincoln's dirty deeds and then became his right-hand-gal because she honestly believed he had something to do with Malorie's disappearance. If she was still being held somewhere, like some of the other girls he had taken, she could hurt your sister to punish you. Once Malorie was found alive and well, the next best thing she could do is get close to Dougie so she could hurt him to make you pay for the sins she believed you committed."

I feel sick.

"So she tried to ruin all three of our lives, and none of us even knew about her? If I didn't know he was married, those two women damn sure didn't either. They only thought he was cheating on me, I'm certain."

My nausea intensifies when I think of what would have happened if Lincoln *was* the one holding Mal hostage. She would have survived all those years just for Chelsey to hurt or kill her to punish me. I would have never gotten my sister back. I search Nelson's office for a trash can, and he snatches the one under his desk and hands it over after reading the panic in my eyes and the slight swaying of my body. I don't throw up, but I stay kneeled on his carpet, hunched over the small can, for at least five minutes while he rubs my back as amicably as possible.

I turn my head slowly because too much motion is going to push me over the edge. He backs away from me and sits back down but keeps his elbows leaned forward on his knees to observe at a safe distance. "Jackie's brother . . . and Alison's mom . . . did they survive?" I ask.

"He's in a coma, but the activity on his brain scans have been encouraging. Unfortunately, Alison's mother succumbed to her injuries. It's been all over the news in the Lansing area because she was quite active in the community."

The memory comes flooding back to me of Alison taking a call from her mother on our way to Chicago. She answered it on speakerphone so I could hear how overprotective she was, but all it did was make me miss my own mother when she repeated her warning to stay in the "right areas" of town and to "never leave your drinks unattended" while out at the bars. She was a sweet woman, and it was obvious she loved her daughter very much. It was another senseless fucking tragedy attributed to Chelsey, one of our resident psychopaths.

"It's one thing that this woman is deranged enough to hurt us because we were involved with Dave, but what about the girls she helped Lincoln keep underground? You're telling me her motive was to go along with his sick crimes in case he had Malorie hidden somewhere?"

My nausea has passed, and now I'm just angry. I slide the trash can back in Nelson's direction and rub my sore knees as I pull myself back up on the padded chair across from him.

"It's not an answer anyone ever wants to hear, but I've taken enough courses in criminology to tell you there are people in this world who aren't right in the head. There are people who commit crimes for the thrill of it and those who completely lack empathy. The darkest criminals of all are the hardest to understand because they don't have clear motives for the heinous things they do. Katie, these people need to be separated from society as soon as humanly possible because they'll never stop destroying innocent lives until they're caught."

Twenty-Two

TONIGHT IT'S JUST LOU, Mal, Deb, and me at the dinner table. Everyone else is either at work or otherwise engaged. I've just told them everything that Nelson told me today, and I'm currently being met with blank stares.

"There's no fucking way," Mal says.

"Language," Deb whispers out of habit.

"I'm nearly forty," Mal responds, and Deb shrugs.

"This little maniac nearly killed Douglas because she was trying to get back at you for sleeping with a man you didn't even know was married?" Lou asks, picking her fork back up. She had dropped onto her plate with a clang when I delivered the news.

"Why does everyone keep referring to him as the man I was sleeping with? I'm not some floozy; he was my fiancé, for crying out loud," I say. "Not that it matters now, I guess."

"But she was on the tapes helping Lincoln. You're telling me she was just passing the time until she could get to you by being an accomplice to kidnapping, assault, and murder?" Mal asks.

Oh, boy. This is going to be hard news to break.

"Well don't fly off the handle because this hasn't been proven yet, but the running theory based on some interviews that they've done with the Palmer's crew is that she was staying close to Lincoln because she thought he had you. It was too much of a coincidence that you went missing, and he had a casual after-school hobby of holding missing girls for extended periods of time. If she could get to you . . . she could hurt you to hurt me."

Deb gasps and Lou looks like she's going to shit a brick. Tears are forming in the corner of Mal's eyes.

"They have to catch her," she says, barely audibly.

"They'll catch her. She's not that smart," Lou says, shoveling a forkful of pasta in her mouth. "She'll fuck up. They always do."

"And Dennis? Do you ever think they'll catch him?" I ask.

Lou takes a few more bites of pasta before answering. She's not in the habit of lying to me, so I'm sure she's trying to come up with a gentle way to tell me that man is gone, and no police force is going to put the manpower into finding him without possessing hard evidence of his involvement with Palmer.

"I'll be honest with you, kid. I'm not sure how high on the priority list it is for the coppers to go after him until they have more dirt on the asshole."

There's no use arguing with that logic, so I lean forward to grab the open bottle of red blend from the center of the table and pour myself a second glass. Deb and I are the only ones drinking wine tonight because Lou likes a glass of whole milk with her pasta, and Mal has another headache. I've been bothering her enough about her headaches, so she's finally agreed to go to the doctor this week. I told her I'd drive her, and we could make a day out of it with shopping and lunch in Marquette.

"How did it go with Dalia and Nicole today?" I ask Mal, changing the subject.

"Surprisingly well," Mal replies. "Dalia is so damned calm all the time, even when the people around her are chaotic. I think her energy rubbed off on Nicole. She relaxed enough to just let it all out. I don't want to tell too much of her business, so I'll let you ask her about it yourself."

That's a fair thing for her to say, and I'm sure Nicole would appreciate her discretion. I'll give her a day or so before asking about it, but if she did open up to Dalia, I hope it gave her enough relief to prove the positive effects of therapy. I don't ask any follow up questions because Lou and Deb still don't know the story of Nicole stumbling upon Mal in the basement years ago and being gaslit into believing it was all a figment of her imagination; they simply believe they had a therapy session to heal their relationship after what Rich did. He took twenty years from my sister, but I know deep down she'd never blame Nicole for the actions of her father. We'd sure hate to be held accountable for the actions of ours.

"When does Nolan leave for his little press tour?" Deb asks.

"Tomorrow morning, and he'll be back right before Christmas. His parents have actually been wanting to come to Grady so they can see the resort," I throw in as casually as possible. It doesn't work; all three women gasp.

"Meeting the parents? That's huge, KB!" Mal says, pinching my arm like she did when we were kids. I swat her away and pretend it didn't hurt, also like when we were kids.

"Could they come for Christmas? They could join us for family dinner at the restaurant if they want. We have a few vacant cabins; they could stay all week," Lou says, and her usual monotone gruff voice has a hint of excitement I haven't heard from her in years.

"Wow, you guys really like this one, eh?" I say, looking around the table to see each of them nodding in agreement.

They never went out of their way to ask Dave to bring his family north, that's for sure.

Lou stands to retrieve a cheesecake Brenda made from the fridge just as Dougie comes in the door of the lodge. "Hey, Douglas, where ya been?" she says, pointing to the pot of pasta on the stove. "Help yourself if you're hungry."

He throws his keys on the counter and grabs a bowl down from the cabinet. "I was actually hanging out with Chuck, if you must know," he says and shoots a victorious look in our direction.

"Don't act like hanging out with Dad is some big prize, Dougie," I tease.

"What were you guys doing?" Mal asks.

"We just played pool at the Moose for a few hours and talked. He wanted to make sure I was okay with everything, I guess."

Dougie scoops a heaping pile of pasta in his bowl, spilling a few noodles and sauce on the counter in the process. He doesn't wipe it up because it's Dougie; he thinks the counters just magically get cleaned each night by the cleaning fairy.

"How *are* you doing with all that, kid?" Lou asks.

"We're always here if you need to talk," Deb adds.

He takes a moment to answer, first grabbing a slice of garlic bread from the sheet pan, a fork from the drawer, and taking his seat at the table. "I've always known he's a piece of shit. Sure, I let myself get excited when he texts me every year on my birthday, but it doesn't change the fact that he's a deadbeat. I just didn't know he was capable of . . . hurting girls. I can't think about it too much or I feel sick."

"You and Nicole have both had a rough year when it comes to finding out some horrible things about your fathers," Deb says, leaning over to rub Dougie's arm. "I bet you could find a lot of common ground if you spent some time together. She'd be a great person if you need someone to lend an ear."

"You trying to hook me up with Nicole, Aunt Deb? She bats for the other team," Dougie says with a smirk before shoveling a forkful of pasta into his mouth, which mostly makes it to his destination, minus a few drops on his chin and shirt.

"Why is everything a joke with you kids? I just thought it would be nice if you two leaned on each other, that's all."

"You're right, Deb. He should spend some time with Nicole. Lou, maybe you could schedule them some shifts together in the kitchen next week, and I'll take his bar shifts," I offer with a sweet smile.

"Like hell you're taking my bar shifts," Dougie replies, shooting me daggers across the table.

"I don't mind all the kitchen shifts," Mal interjects. "It keeps me away from the public, and I'm actually enjoying my shifts with Robbie; he cracks me up. I feel bad that he's not getting along with his parents; he's just such a good kid."

Twenty-Three

MAL'S three high school friends came back over this morning, and Lou cooked a big breakfast for everyone. I stole a few slices of bacon and a cinnamon roll and took them in my bedroom so I could call Nolan and talk to him while he's on the road. His first tour stop is a podcast convention in downtown Chicago, and he just received news that he and Karli are the only "talent" to sell out their meet-and-greet passes, which was surreal news for him. The more I get to know him, the prouder I am. Everyone and their brother seem to think they can host a successful show these days, but Nolan really puts in the work. He cares about the victims and their families more than any journalist I've interacted with in the last twenty years.

After hanging up with Nolan, I decided there was no harm in being a little nosey, so I sat in my room with the door cracked, eavesdropping on Mal and her friends. There was a lot of laughter, which put my soul at ease. Mal needs laughter. There was a bit of awkwardness when the girls would reference something that happened while Mal was gone, but she brushed it off with her signature sarcasm. I listened to the girls fill her in on all the major life events that happened while she was held captive. Everyone was so focused on how we were doing as a family when Mal disappeared, I'm ashamed to admit not many of us worried enough about her friends. These are the girls she spent every day at school with and then most nights either at Johnny's Pizza or somewhere by the water causing harmless trouble. They were all about to leave for college when one of them vanished into thin air, and the other three were just supposed to pack up and move into their respective dorms, going on with life as usual. It guts me that none of us acknowledged how hard that must have been.

When the girls say their goodbyes, I reappear in the kitchen to help Mal clean up the mess so we can get on the road to Marquette for her doctor's appointment. It's basically a wellness appointment so her doctor can verify that she's gaining enough weight and her eyesight is back to normal, but she promised she's going to mention the headaches and random bouts of sweating she's been experiencing. I personally think they are mild panic attacks, but I'm not a doctor.

"Are you glad they came over?" I ask.

"I am," she replies, but I can tell there's more she wants to say, so I tilt my head with a scrunched nose so she'll keep going. "I know this is silly, but it sounds like I missed out on a lot of heartache. The stories they told today were about miscarriages, cheating, divorce, health scares . . . I know I missed out, but I guess I dodged a bullet with some coming-of-age moments."

I yet again open my mouth when I'm certain Dalia would not approve of my question, but I can't help myself.

"Do you ever think about meeting someone and getting married in the future? I hope that's not a silly question to ask."

Malorie stops scrubbing the pan in her hands and momentarily stares off in the distance.

"The first few months down there, I'd still get butterflies

in my stomach thinking about Lincoln. That makes me want to vomit now, but at the time . . . I thought I loved him. Rich would tell me stories about what a horrible man he was, but I thought he was lying so he could poison my idea of him. After I lost the baby, my love for Lincoln faded a little more every day, and I just kind of lost interest in men altogether. Even when I was able to watch *Entertainment Tonight* and they'd be talking about Hollywood's latest heartthrob, I'd look at their faces and feel nothing. Now that I'm free, I guess I'm just waiting to see if I'll ever feel fondness for a man like that again. Maybe I'm broken."

"You're not broken, Mal. Far from it. You just need some time to figure out what you want, that's all. You're not even forty; you still have plenty of time," I assure her. It breaks my heart that those thoughts are even crossing her mind.

"Maybe I'll just stay single forever like the aunts," she declares. She's standing at the sink with her back to me, but I see her shake her head when she says it.

"That wouldn't be the end of the world; they don't have to deal with anyone's shit. If it doesn't work out with Nolan, I'm tempted to do the same."

She turns her head to the side so I can see her smile. We spend the next ten minutes cleaning the kitchen in silence before freshening up for our little road trip to Marquette.

"Maybe we can listen to Nolan's podcast on the way?" she asks as we are getting into my SUV.

"Well of course. Which season?" I ask.

"Mine," she says after buckling her seatbelt.

"Are you sure you want to do that? The first few episodes are interviews with all of us before we knew you were still alive. It might get kind of emotional."

She considers it for a minute before nodding in confirmation and saying, "Okay, that's fair. Skip to the episode where

I'm alive. It's the most popular podcast in America. I just want to see what all the fuss is about."

"Fair enough." I smile before scrolling to the right episode and clicking play. I already had it pulled up on Spotify because I've been listening to it on repeat. The joy in Nolan's voice when he starts the episode with the news that Malorie is alive and well makes my whole body feel warm. It's not often he gets to deliver good news in his line of work.

* * *

Mal's appointment is taking longer than I expected, but I have no idea why that is because she wouldn't let me go back in the examination room with her. I'm in the waiting area with a couple around our age and their three children. The youngest is wailing, the middle is slamming a toy truck into the edge of a wooden coffee table—much to the displeasure of the woman working the front desk—and the oldest is asking his mother approximately one hundred questions regarding the doctor's office and what they're doing there. The husband? Watching golf on television. I couldn't make this up if I tried. This poor woman is doing all she can to keep it together, and he can't be bothered to look away from the screen mounted on the wall for a minute.

It's not that I dislike children; I've just never been around them, so I'm not sure how to entertain them. I take my chances by setting my magazine aside and getting down on my knees next to the noisy toddler, who is playing "smash the truck" alone at the coffee table in front of him. I retrieve a plastic racetrack from the toy bin between us and click the parts together to form a figure eight. A few sample runs with matchbox cars around the loops and he's mesmerized; he takes the cars from my hands and races them around the track. Although he's making a low humming sound to mimic the engine noises, it's much quieter than the constant banging of his metal truck against the edge of the table. His mother mouths *thank you* just as her oldest turns his attention to me and begins to rapid-fire ask me about who I am and why I'm here. She stands to run interference, but I subtly shake my head. I feel like I haven't done enough good deeds lately, and if distracting these two so she can have a moment to focus on her newborn will win me some karma points, I'm happy to be of service.

I reach for an old Benard's Lakeside Inn pen from the bottom of my bag and rip off the blank bottom half from my grocery list before setting it on the table between us.

"I bet you love to draw. Is there any chance you would draw me a picture?" I ask.

"I guess," he mumbles, snatching the pen from my hand.

The baby's screams have now quieted to labored breathing from exhaustion, and the two older boys are preoccupied with their tasks. Just as I raise my head to shoot a disgusted look at the father, my sister comes out of the door next to the front desk. Her eyes are red and swollen.

"I'm sorry, I've got to go," I tell the mother and she gives me an appreciative smile.

I get back on my feet and grab my bag just in time to catch my sister pushing the door open to leave the doctor's office. As I'm walking out the door, I hear the oldest child ask his mother where I'm going and why I didn't wait for him to finish the picture, so I turn my head to apologize just as the middle child picks his toy truck back up and slams it full throttle into his father's kneecap. He spews a few cuss words that a toddler should never hear, and my eyes shoot over to his wife who, just for a split second, meets my gaze and smiles.

Twenty-Four

"TAKE a deep breath and tell me everything," I say once we are settled in the safety of my car. She hasn't said a word, but she began to sob once we hit the parking lot, and it was so unusual to see this reaction from my steel-nerved sister, I couldn't come up with a word to say. I just wrapped my arm around her while we walked slowly to my car, my eyes darting around the property for journalists and thankfully seeing none.

"I promised Dalia I would never focus on the unfairness of it all. We all have bad things happen to us in life, and if I focus too much on all that has been taken from me, I'll miss out on all the beautiful things waiting," she tells me, wiping her face with a few fast-food napkins I had stored in my glovebox.

"Are you . . . sick? Whatever it is Mal, we'll get through it. There are so many advances in modern medicine. Whatever it is, we can fight it and win," I tell her.

She laughs, but it's more of a pity laugh like I can't possibly understand what she's going through.

"My headaches, sweats, irritability . . . she thinks it's possible that I'm entering early menopause. Mom started showing symptoms in her late-thirties as well. They are going to test my hormones to see what's going on, but that's her gut feeling. I'm in perimenopause."

Ignorantly, my first instinct is relief. We all go through menopause if we are lucky enough to live that long. It's just part of life. I don't take the time to realize what this really means until she spells it out for me.

"He took it from me, Katie. He took my ability to be a mother. If my baby would have been born in a hospital, and I would have had the medical care I needed throughout my pregnancy, she could have survived. Now my body probably can't even sustain a pregnancy. It's too late. He wasted my childbearing years and I can never get them back."

What can you say when your heart crumbles into pieces for someone else? It didn't occur to me that Mal ever wanted to be a mother, and it surely never occurred to me that it could be too late. I just turned thirty-six and she's about to be thirty-nine. I feel like we are the picture of youth. Perimenopause wasn't even in my vocabulary.

"You could adopt, Mal. There are so many kids who need good homes," I tell her because it's the only consolation I can think of.

"I'm sure the agencies are dying to approve a single woman with no career who's been locked in a basement for two decades. Where do I find the application?"

I put my hand over hers and stare out my windshield at the traffic passing by the hospital. "We'll figure something out. We always do."

After sitting in the car for a few more minutes and discussing her options, Mal tells me she still wants to shop and grab lunch because that's what we came here for. She reaches in the backseat for her baseball cap and sunglasses. There's always a chance that it's overkill and nobody will recognize her, but there's also a chance that they will.

We start at Ulta and TJ Maxx, which both go smoothly. She spends a total of one hundred and twenty-five dollars and keeps musing about how she feels like Oprah. I point out that she now has a bank account with more zeroes than I've seen in my life, and she reminds me that the last time she went shopping, one hundred dollars was a lot of money.

Nobody bothers her, nobody stares, nobody gives her so much as a second glance. I feel my shoulders tense each time someone slows their pace near us, but they each just flip through a rack or check price tags. Our luck runs out shortly after we enter Target, but the woman is quiet and respectful as she leans toward Mal in the bedding section and whispers, "We're all so glad you're home."

I choose The Vierling for lunch because the water view is breathtaking, the food is always delicious, and I know the weekday daytime host so she'll hook us up with a private table in the back. Luckily, I don't even need to ask – Megan, an old employee of Benard's back when she lived on the lake, gives me a hug, introduces herself to Malorie with zero awkwardness, and gives me a wink before leading us to a corner table. Mal sits with her back to the restaurant, which makes me happy because it gives her the best view of Lake Superior. The waves are crashing so violently today, it looks like the ocean. Winter is on its way.

It is embarrassingly obvious that Megan has spoken to our server and explained the situation because she's nervous, overly polite, and doing her best to avoid eye contact with Mal. My sister shakes her head slightly with a smile before telling the server, "I know it's probably a little weird waiting on me because everyone thought I was dead, but it's okay, I promise. My sister keeps telling me how good the food is here, so I plan to come here a lot. It would be great if you could be our regular server."

It's like someone pulled a pin out of her back and all the

tension that was keeping her shoulders and jaw tight simply deflates from relief. "I can't tell you how nervous I was to greet your table," she admits.

Her service is smooth as butter for the next hour – our drinks are never empty, and she delivers our entrees the minute we finish our salads. I'm not sure if we are her only table, but we're being treated like it. Mal and I talk about Dougie, Nicole, Dennis, Chelsey – all of it. It feels like we are in high school again, just grabbing lunch and losing ourselves in conversation until it's time to go back to real life.

I pay the check, even though Mal now has a net worth of six figures, and we head back to the car to return to Grady.

"You're the best sister I could ever ask for," she tells me as I pull out of our parking spot.

"I knew we shouldn't have ordered dessert; it always makes you sentimental." I tease.

"I can't wait to get back home; I'm going to take a two-hour nap," Mal says absentmindedly while reaching back to set her leftovers behind the passenger seat and fastening her seatbelt.

Good, I think. That will give me the perfect opportunity to drive to the Grady Jail and see Rich Lowery so I can slap him across the face for yet another thing he's taken from my sister. I've avoided him long enough.

Twenty-Five

"THAT'S JUST NOT how things work, KB."

Mike Robinson, my former classmate and current Grady Jail employee is trying to explain to me why I can't just go back to Rich's cell and have a little chat with him. I'm refusing to hear anything he has to say because the more I thought about everything he's done on the drive home from Marquette, the more furious I became. I think I've been holding back all month for Nicole's sake and also because I was just so happy to have my sister home. Now that the dust is settling, I think I might kill him.

"I just want to ask him a few questions. How does that affect your job in any way?" I ask him.

Mike chokes out a condescending laugh. "You can't be serious – how would it affect my job? I'd *lose* my job, KB. The Sheriff went home for the night. I can't just let anyone who walks in here go hang out with the prisoners. Not on my watch."

"Anyone who walks in here? We've known each other our entire lives," I remind him. When that doesn't succeed in busting down his defenses, I try a different tactic. "Look, his sentencing is Monday and then he'll be transferred to a prison that might not even be in the state of Michigan. This could be my last chance to see him face-to-face."

"What's all this about?" Sheriff Nelson half-shouts as he comes down the hall toward us.

"Sir, I'm sorry. I thought you went home for the night," Mike says with a slight quiver in his voice.

"Oh, don't blame him. I was just trying to have a word with Rich before he gets transferred but *Michael* here was just explaining to me that it's against your policy to let me back there."

Nelson looks from Mike to me and back again before running a hand over his two-day stubble. "Son, you did the right thing. I'll take it from here."

Mike looks at me nervously before nodding his hat to Nelson and leaving us alone in the hallway.

"What do you want with Rich Lowery, young lady?"

"I just want to ask him a few questions. This could be my last chance," I say with pleading eyes. "I just need a few minutes, I promise."

"It's more than a little unorthodox to allow the victim's family to visit with the man convicted of kidnapping their sister. This is all in addition to it being well past visiting hours."

"The victim's family? It's me, Sheriff. It's just me and I just need a few minutes with him for closure. Please."

He chews on it for a minute before giving in.

"I'll set him up in the interrogation room at the end of the hall on the right. Give me a few minutes for the transport and then I'll come get you from the waiting room. You know, the waiting room up front where most visitors stay until they're told they can come back?"

I ignore his wisecrack because I'm so focused on the news that I'm going to see Rich. I'm going to see the son of a bitch who stole so much from my family. I quickly agree and return to the front of the building to wait for Nelson to retrieve me. Every once in a while, I experience a wave of gratitude for being from this small town where rules can be bent when they needed to be. If we were in a bigger city, there's not a chance in hell I'd be getting facetime with the man who kidnapped my sister.

For the next ten minutes, I sit in an uncomfortable metal chair and mentally rehearse everything I'm going to say to him. I want my words to play over and again in his mind as he's transferred to prison, where the conditions won't be cushy like the Grady Jail.

"Alright, KB. Let's go. You've got ten minutes. No touching, no spitting, no yelling. I mean it. Don't make me regret this."

I give my sincerest promise and follow Nelson down the dimly lit hall to the back room on the right, labeled Interrogation Room B. I wonder what's going on in room A causing him to choose room B, but I don't focus on it long because I've got work to do. I'm going to find out where the bastard buried Mal's baby so she can have an ounce of the closure she deserves.

What I'm struck by most when I enter the room is that Rich looks healthy. He doesn't look tired or hungry or abused, like most men would after their first month in jail. He looks well-fed and content. This intensifies my urge to jump across the table and strangle him, but I resist. I have questions I need answered.

"Hey, kid," he greets me with the moniker he's been calling me most of my life.

"Hey, you piece of shit. I guess I didn't need to feel guilty all those years for being the reason you were investigated for her disappearance. I only regret that they didn't look harder," I say with such vitriol my hands immediately begin to shake.

"Hey now," Nelson yells with a thunderous knock to the small window. I'm not sure if he heard me through the door or if he has a listening device in the room. I also don't really care.

"Katie, I've been a very troubled man and I've got a lot of mental issues that need to be treated. Once I came to my senses about Malorie, it was too late. I was in too deep," Rich says calmly, as if he's prepared for this interaction more than I have.

"I don't need to hear your fucking excuses. She's alive and we're going to make up for lost time and give her the most beautiful life she's ever dreamed of. You will be a distant memory that grows smaller in her mind as each day passes, you fucking monster."

He flinches.

"I'm sorry, Rich. Did you expect to receive warmth and kindness from the sister of the woman you kept in your basement for two decades? Is that what you think you deserve?"

He dramatically exhales, drops his gaze down to his hands and begins to pick at his cuticles. "What is it that you want, Katie Benard?"

"I have three questions for you. If you'll answer them, I'll leave and make sure none of my family members show up to your sentencing to protest the absolute bullshit agreement that's going to allow you to be up for parole in twenty years. I'll also make sure Nicole is welcome at every holiday gathering we have so she'll never feel alone."

This gets his attention. Apparently even monsters have a soft spot for their offspring. He nods for me to continue.

"Tell me what you know about my Uncle Dennis' involvement with Lincoln."

"Exactly what I told Nelson – I couldn't believe it when I saw him on those tapes with Palmer. I'd known Dennis my entire life. Sure, he was an asshole with a gambling problem, but the worst thing I'd ever seen him do was get a little phys-

ical with Brenda. I took him out to my cabin to cool off, and
—"

"He got physical with Aunt Brenda? Like he hit her?" I interrupt. He stares back at me like I'm the only idiot in Grady to be in the dark about this abuse.

"Ahh . . . yeah, I mean . . . they had some heated arguments. Nothing I hadn't seen before. But I never got the feeling that he was some sort of pedophile, which is why I was so shocked to see him with those girls on the land. I had my entire speech worked out to confront him and talk some sense into him, but he never showed up on the cams again. In fact, he skipped town shortly after and I always felt that Brenda must have threatened to file a police report on him because he was slapping her around. He never came back to face the music. That blonde girl from Palmer's Resort is the one the cops need to focus on. I had a bad feeling about her before I even realized it was her on the tapes. That girl's got something seriously wrong with her."

I fully understand how ludicrous this sounds, but I believe him. Rich is speaking to me like he's talking to an old fishing buddy, and he answered me immediately, without having to think of a lie. My guard is up, but I somehow believe that Dougie's dad was only on the tapes in the early days and then came to his senses. I didn't know there was any domestic abuse, but I was also young and naïve and couldn't imagine any man in my family laying their hands on a female. I'm assuming it's a decently kept secret because he wouldn't have survived Lou finding out he was abusing her little sister.

I hate myself for asking this next question, because it means that deep down, I need confirmation before giving Nicole my full trust.

"Did you trick your daughter into thinking that she didn't really see Mal in your basement room?"

His head jerks up violently, eyes wide. He can't believe Nicole confessed this to me.

"I wasn't in my right mind, Katie. I've told you this. Nic was having all sorts of trouble on that medication, I still think Doc Irving prescribed her too much. It was messing with her head, which made it easy to convince her she was seeing things."

His lips curl when the realization hits. "You're asking me this because you didn't believe Nicole when she told you."

"I believe Nicole, she's my best friend. I just wanted to hear it directly from you that you gaslit your own daughter into believing she didn't see Malorie. That's pretty fucked up, yet it's not even in the top five worst things you've done. I know about my mother."

"I loved your mother," he tells me.

"You let my mother die on the floor of your basement while her oldest daughter watched. That's love?"

"It was complicated," he says, and I have to direct my mind elsewhere or my lip will start to tremble before the tears fall. I know it's not healthy, but not thinking of my mother's death at all has been the best way to cope. I'll drive myself crazy if I think of the unfairness of it all. I'm sure Dalia would have a thing or two to say about my coping mechanisms. "What's the third question?" he asks.

"Where the fuck is Malorie's baby buried and what could you possibly have to lose at this point by just telling us so we can have a proper burial?"

He starts shaking his head so rapidly, it's as if his body is having a physical reaction to my question.

"Trust me when I say it's better you don't know."

"And trust me when I say, we're already assuming the worst of you so if the issue is that you smothered the baby, nobody is going to be surprised. I'll talk to the family and see what I can do about agreeing to recommend immunity to the prosecutor if you'll just give us the location."

"I didn't smother any babies. I've never killed anyone in my life. I know that's hard for you to believe."

"So tell us where the body is."

"I don't expect you to understand what goes on in my brain, but my intentions were always to protect people. I gave my mother the apartment above the Grab N Go so she could retire with a lake view and gossip with the locals, which was her favorite thing to do. I have supported every crazy idea Nicole has ever had. I believed I was protecting Malorie from Lincoln Palmer, and maybe I did save her life. We know what that man was capable of; who says he wouldn't have killed her to prevent her from having that baby?"

He's not wrong. Who the hell knows what that man was capable of?

"You robbed Mal of the opportunity to be a mother. I'll never forgive you for that."

Something passes between us and for a minute, I almost think he's going to disagree with that statement. I'm glad he keeps his mouth shut because I'm not in the mood to explain Malorie's biological clock to him.

"Please, just answer me so we can give the baby the funeral she deserves. It's quite literally the very least you could do for our family."

"You don't need to have a funeral," he mumbles before motioning to the window that he's done with this conversation. "Tell Malorie I'm sorry."

Twenty-Six

IT'S NEARLY midnight when my phone lights up with a call from Nolan. Mal and I are sitting up in our respective beds, eyes glued to the new TV we just bought for our room. We're up entirely too late watching a reality show about couples who propose before physically seeing each other. Everyone online has been talking about it, so I convinced Mal to give it a try, and we haven't been able to peel our eyes from it for hours. I think we're on our fifth or sixth episode straight. It's been a nice distraction, so I can divert my thoughts from my meeting with Rich today. Nobody knows about it except for Mike and Sheriff Nelson, and I plan to keep it that way. I keep replaying Rich's words, *You don't need to have a funeral.* What the hell does this guy think he knows about what my family needs?

"Everything okay?" I answer. Nolan knows I'm usually out cold by ten, so it's unusual for him to call at this hour.

"Hey babe, were you asleep?"

"No, actually Mal and I are watching this trashy show that we can't—"

"Just you and Mal? Can you put me on speakerphone so I can talk to you both?" he interrupts.

I shoot Mal a look. She sets down her second bowl of popcorn and sits up straight as I pull the phone away from my ear and punch the speakerphone button.

"Okay, we're both listening. What's up?"

"This is going to be hard to hear, but I need you to hear it from me first. One of my contacts just called to give me a heads up that one of Mal's friends sold a story to a tabloid. They already published the article online ahead of it going to print, and several blogs have grabbed pieces from it to make clickbait headlines."

Mal's lips twitch up into an uncomfortable smirk while she shakes her head.

"Oh, not *my* friends. I've only seen my three best friends from high school. I haven't talked to anyone else, so they wouldn't have a story to sell. Whatever they told the reporter is probably something they made up to make a few bucks," Mal says, the tone in her voice implying that Nolan should know one of her close friends would never betray her like that. "I'm sure it's some local who is hard on their luck or looking for their fifteen minutes. We can put out a statement and let everyone know that it's all lies."

"It was one of your friends, Mal. She had breakfast with you the other day and recorded you on her phone. The reporter sent me the transcript; you talk about having headaches, about Katie and I dating, and about Chelsey's obsession with your family and how she might be a psycho who is attacking every woman who has slept with Dave. I even hear Katie when she comes in the room to make herself a plate. I'm so sorry."

Mal's head continues to swing back and forth while Nolan speaks, willing the words to be untrue. I listened to a little of the conversation when her friends were over for breakfast, and

I'm certain they talked about all three of these things. Nobody outside of this lodge could know that Malorie was having headaches and, other than law enforcement, I don't think the investigation into Chelsey's motives has been made public. Sure, the locals know about Nolan and me by now, but it hasn't hit any national news or blogs.

"Which one? Which one sold the story?" she asks so low, I'm not sure Nolan hears her.

"I don't know, Malorie. I promise I'll do my best to find out, but part of the deal is usually for the source to have the ability to remain anonymous."

"Can we pay to kill the story? How much would that cost?" I ask, feeling like a high-stakes fixer in an action movie.

"Search my name," Nolan says. "Search my name and click on news results."

I follow his directions, tapping around on my phone until the search results populate. The top hit is from a popular true crime website.

AMERICA'S FAVORITE PODCAST HOST DATING SISTER OF MALORIE ROSE BENARD — CAN YOU SAY CONFLICT OF INTEREST?

The second is from an internet news company that has become everyone's favorite quick and easy way to consume the latest headlines.

NOLAN COWELL SAVES THE LIFE OF MALORIE ROSE BENARD — AND THEN BEDS HER SISTER!

Against my better judgement, I back space his name from the search bar and type in my sister's. I gasp when I read the first few headlines, and Mal snatches the phone from me. I can hear Nolan protesting and telling us to stop reading, but it's too late.

MALORIE ROSE BENARD RESCUED AFTER TWENTY YEARS, ONLY TO BE DIAGNOSED WITH MASSIVE BRAIN TUMOR!

Malorie Rose Vows to Hunt Down Fugitive Chelsey Benoit — Vengeance for the Residents of Small Lakeside Town

Malorie Rose Benard and Only Sister Estranged After Romp with Podcast Host Who Saved Her

Natalie Portman Rumored to Play the Role of Malorie Rose Benard in Netflix Adaption of America's Most Famous Kidnapping

Her eyes stop darting back and forth across the headlines and pause on the floor between us.

"This nightmare is never going to end, is it?"

Twenty-Seven

MY PHONE IS FILLED with alerts by the time I wake up; thank goodness I always sleep with the ringer turned off. I have texts from all three of Mal's high school friends, promising it wasn't them who leaked the recording, each one placing the blame on another. For all I'm concerned, all three of them are guilty, and until we prove otherwise, I hope Mal has zero contact with them. Thank goodness she doesn't have a cell phone yet.

Ever the smart ass, Nicole texted me a screenshot of a headline about Nolan and me and wrote, "You're sleeping with Khaki Pants?! I don't even know you anymore!" followed by, "JK . . . let me know if you need anything. Sorry that people have nothing better to talk about. I wish I could kick all their asses for you, KB."

I have a message from Nolan, sent shortly after seven in the morning, that says, "I'm so sorry I had to call you with the news last night. I hate giving your family any more bad news, ever. The only silver lining, I guess . . ." Below his message is a picture of the top podcast charts on iTunes and Spotify, with

Gone, but Not Forgotten retaking the number one spot on both after falling out of the top ten last week. *Oh, boy.*

I flip over to check on Malorie in her bed across the room, but it's empty. If I already have a headache before getting up, I can't imagine how she feels. I reluctantly get out of bed and perform a few stretches that have become necessary to work the kinks out of my body since the moment I turned thirty-five. It's overcast outside when I open the curtains to our bedroom window, the soft gray clouds hanging low over the rippling lake. We all love the gloomy, moody weather around Halloween and Thanksgiving, but once December hits, we are all ready for a winter wonderland to last through Christmas, so these dark days with no snow on the ground tend to put everyone around here in a sour mood.

After using the bathroom, I tiptoe out of our room because I'm not sure if anyone else is still sleeping. I'm surprised to find only Aunt Deb in the family room, staring out the window at the same view I was just mentally complaining about.

"These gloomy days sure are beautiful," she muses.

"They sure are, Deb." I lie.

"Can I talk to you for a minute, kiddo?" she asks.

"Always. Where is everyone?"

"Douglas is still sleeping and the rest of them are at the restaurant. Mal went in a little early so Robbie could show her how to make the homemade eggnog and Tom and Jerry mixes for the bar. It's December now and once that snow hits, you know how crazy everyone gets for Christmas drinks."

I smile at the mention of Mal being at work with Robbie. I know he'll make her laugh and get her mind off the betrayal committed by one of her oldest friends. Deb pats the cushion of the couch next to her and motions for me to sit down.

"You're one of the strongest kids I know," she says, reaching forward to run her hand through my hair like my mother used to do. "That's why I wanted to talk to you alone."

"You're scaring me, Deb."

She dismisses the comment with a curt laugh.

"I know it seems like this family has had a long string of bad luck lately, but I think everyone has seasons of good and bad luck. We just happen to be in a season of bad. I don't think it's like the Kennedy curse; it's just temporary . . . it always is. After Mal disappeared and your mother died, back-to-back, we thought the sky was falling. But then for years, it was quiet. Sure, we had minor issues, but nothing crazy. We had years of peace."

"I'd have to agree," I say, not knowing exactly where she's going with this. Maybe she just wants to say it out loud to convince herself that our family's luck is about to change. There will be no more kidnappings, assaults, childhood friends selling stories to the press. "Hopefully we're about to enter another season of peace in this family."

"Has anyone ever told you about the Ghosts of Grady?" she asks. Something stirs in me; I've heard this phrase before. I was very young and don't remember the circumstances, only that I overheard someone in the family talking about them, and it scared me half to death. I didn't know what it meant, but I pictured scary ghosts in white sheets hovering over the lake, vacant stares showing through the holes cut out for their eyes. I'm certain it kept me up at night more than once.

When I shake my head, she continues.

"When my grandparents, your great-grandparents, settled here, they built this resort with their own hands. Of course back then, it was only the lodge, restaurant, and four cabins, but they stayed booked. Travelers came from all around the Midwest to spend time at Benard's Lakeside Inn. Al Capone even hung out here; or so I've been told. They had seven great years before prohibition destroyed their entire business.

Grandpa George tried to create a speakeasy type situation, but he wasn't very slick. He got raided several times."

"No way," I interject. "Did he go to jail?"

Deb smiles, shaking her head.

"Back then, Grady Jail only had one cell. They'd hold Grandpa until a more important criminal got arrested, and the Sheriff would drop him back off at the resort with a stern warning not to do it again."

"Well, that doesn't seem like a string of bad luck for the Benards; it was bad luck for everyone. Prohibition wasn't just a problem for them," I point out.

"I'm sure you've heard stories of the root cellar that got filled in shortly before your grandparents took over," she says.

"Yeah . . . over where cabin five is, right? It was underground storage for the dry goods before they built onto the restaurant and added the dry storage room."

"That's where my grandpa had the speakeasy. It only held about ten men at once, but it was underground and could hold plenty of bootlegged liquor. It was a pretty successful side hustle, until a woman was found dead in the cellar."

"What?" I gasp. "Who was she?"

"Let's just say she was a woman of ill repute."

"Ill repute . . . a prostitute?" I am floored. A prostitute in Grady? A prostitute found dead in my family's root cellar? How have I never heard about this? "Did your grandpa have something to do with it?" I ask.

"From what I've been told, he didn't. He was a hardworking, stand-up guy who loved my grandmother very much. The woman was reportedly killed by a local attorney with enough money to bury the entire situation. Grandma and Grandpa were so grief-stricken by what happened they locked up the root cellar and almost went out of business from the lack of extra income. Dad told me that they nearly starved to death one winter and would regularly go over a month without a single customer. Then prohibition finally ended, business slowly got back to normal, my grandparents retired a few years later, and my parents took over the resort."

I furrow my brow, knowing there's more to her story.

"The fall that my parents decided to build on cabins five through eight, business was good. It was better than good, actually. They were just finishing the busiest tourist season on record; everyone was overjoyed. They even started paying us kids to help out at the resort instead of using us a free child labor. One morning, Dad went down by the lake to check on the construction of the new cabins. That's when he saw a small child entering the water near the north cove."

I shiver, knowing where this is going. I've heard variations of this tale since I was in elementary school.

"He couldn't make it there soon enough. They say the November winds got the little boy. He was the son of one of the construction workers, on the job with his dad because his mother had fallen ill and they didn't have any other family in Michigan to help. It took hours to recover his tiny, little body."

Before the kids were haunted by the disappearance of Malorie Rose Benard, my generation was terrorized by the story of Little Billy who drowned in Grady Lake. The older kids would tell us that we couldn't swim after dark because it made Billy mad, and he'd pull us under. He was the first casualty of the lake on record, and the lore was strong.

"Mom and Dad were wrecked. They stopped construction until spring. They barely made it through Christmas. I'll never forget the night that my grandpa sat them down and told them about the Ghosts of Grady. He said every twenty years or so, the residents of Grady Lake experience unspeakable tragedy with no reasonable explanation as to why. His best guess is that they chose questionable land to build the resort on—land that meant something to the former residents of the lake, most likely early settlers whose spirits are not happy with all the development. He said there's nothing you can do except keep to yourself and wait for the ghosts to pass and then enjoy your good fortune while they're gone."

"Why are you telling me all of this?" I ask her. She stares in my eyes like she'd rather be doing anything else than telling me what she's about to say, but she knows she *has* to say it.

"The end of each cycle of the Ghosts of Grady has been signified by a great sickness. I know it sounds silly now, but Grandpa always thought the bad luck was manifesting in the form of an illness, and when the host dies, the bad luck is over."

"That's pretty morbid," I say.

"When prohibition ended, Grandma felt ill for days and then died in her sleep. After everyone grieved, life got better in Grady. After that little boy's death, that's when Dad got cancer. He was dead within six months and then the family led a peaceful existence until years later when Malorie was kidnapped. Your mother died of an undiagnosed heart condition, and then we saw some peace again. It's become a routine in this family—bad luck, illness, death, and then a break from it all. The only mercy those ghosts ever show this family is letting us catch our breath before they come back to wreak havoc."

"So what are you saying?" I ask. "Do you think one of us is going to get sick and die?"

"I have cancer, Katie Bug. I know that's not the news you want to hear, but I'm telling you first because I know you'll understand. It's not a reason to be sad. It's a reason to celebrate because it means the ghosts will leave us alone soon."

Twenty-Eight

AFTER DEB TELLS the rest of the family about her diagnosis, the next few weeks feel like some sort of fucked-up version of *Groundhog Day*.

At least once a day, someone bursts into tears about Deb's cancer. It's usually Brenda, but I did see Lou furiously wipe away a tear while reading the informational printout that the doctor in Marquette gave Deb to bring home. The prognosis isn't great.

Malorie goes back and forth between wanting to confront her friends about their betrayal and just cutting them out of her life completely and pretending they don't exist. She's replayed the morning she spent with them over and over and told me her intuition is saying it was Taylor, her divorced, single-mother friend who lives in Marquette. Mal has no reason other than "a gut feeling," which happens to be good enough for me. She wants more time to think before deciding what to do about it and says her time is better spent focused on Deb, anyway.

Nolan has been on the road for his press tour, so our relationship has survived solely on texts and occasional Facetime calls when he can find a quiet moment. Used to the discretion of businesses in Chicago, Nolan was reminded of how small towns operate when he called our only florist to order me a winter bouquet. The owner, Curt, a guy I went to school with, responded, "Oh, dope. You must be the podcast dude. KB will love these."

Dougie is trying his best to reconcile that the woman he thought he was beginning a sweet little romance with and his biological father are both on the run to avoid going to prison for their unspeakable acts. Nelson has been kind enough to give us daily updates on their search, even when there's not much of an update to give. He assures us that apprehending Dennis and Chelsey are top priorities, but it's likely he's only saying that to pacify the family. Dougie attempts to call the last number Dennis texted him from at least once a week, but it's disconnected, and I don't have the heart to tell him that's probably not going to change.

Nobody is surprised when JoAnne Palmer gets a sweetheart deal due to her money, influence, and her claims that Lincoln was abusive and controlling. A year of probation and serving her community at a battered women's shelter, and she'll be a free woman.

Nicole is doing a little better, believe it or not. She and Karli text every day and have plans to hang out over Christmas. The families of Lincoln Palmer's victims have settled with his estate for an undisclosed amount of money and apparently have no interest in seeking ownership of Rich's land where the bunkers are buried. Rich was able to sign the land, the cabin, and the store over to Nicole, since my family won't be going after him in civil court. We have no interest in taking a dime from Nicole; she's been through enough. Rich signed away the next twenty years of his life with his plea deal, and if there's any justice in this universe, he'll die before his release day comes.

Lieutenant Barkley has gone back downstate, but I've overheard Lou on the phone with him several times. She says she's just checking progress on the investigation, but I know better. She always smokes a cigarette when they hang up and stares out at the lake with a look that's unusual for her—a genuine smile.

The first week after Mal's conversation got leaked was absolute pandemonium, and we even considered closing the restaurant for a few days. Luckily, our other employees took over so we could hide in the lodge and wait until another story grabbed the nation's attention, as it always does. Robbie has even grown quite protective of Malorie, regularly chasing reporters off the property and threatening lawsuits that make absolutely no sense. *I'll sue you for even asking about her! When the lawyers are done with you, you won't even have any shoes left!* Sweet Robbie, his heart is in the right place. He's fitting in with this family just fine.

Here we are now, two days before Christmas, and there is finally snow on the ground. Grady Lake looks like a winter postcard that's far too beautiful to be real. This is the weather we've all been waiting for. Nolan should be pulling into town any minute, and he's bringing his parents with. I haven't met them yet, but I nearly had a heart attack when he gave his mother my phone number to call and ask about what she can contribute to our family dinner. She seemed lovely, and the Benards have promised to be on their best behavior when the Bowens, Nolan's mom and stepdad, arrive. There's no guessing what Nicole may do, but having a wild card for a best friend is simply the hand I was dealt.

Last week, Chelsey Benoit was officially named as the prime suspect in the attacks on the family members of Dave's other lovers, as well as on Dougie. They have yet to officially announce her connection to Sammie's mysterious drowning because they don't want to cause anymore unnecessary stress on her parents until they're certain. I've been looking for any other reason as to why she would want to hurt my cousin because it's nearly too much to bear to admit that he almost died because of me. I've been thinking a lot about Chelsey's motivation. When it comes to crimes this severe and calculated, I believe that some humans simply lack empathy, some have a distorted view of logic, and others are just pure evil. Chelsey checks all three boxes, and until she's apprehended, I'll always have my guard up, waiting for the day she returns to Grady.

Dave has tried to call a few times to apologize for what he inadvertently put my family through, but I don't have anything to say to him, so I just send the calls to voicemail. In a rare moment of lightheartedness in these past few weeks, I showed Mal a trend on TikTok where users record themselves doing silly dances with voicemails from their exes playing in the background. Although she wouldn't let me record, she did a fantastic performance to Dave's latest three-minute message, and we collapsed on the floor in laughter.

Now, I'm in cabin two, fluffing pillows for the third time this morning because I've run out of things to do to make sure this place is perfect for the arrival of Nolan's parents. Nicole gave me a four-foot Christmas tree out of storage to place in the corner, so they feel cozy while away from home for the holiday. With its sparkling twinkly lights and white flocked branches, it's pure magic next to the large window overlooking the lake. I've also stocked the cupboards with their favorite coffee, sweeteners, and packets of oatmeal, thanks to Nolan's suggestions. He'll be staying in the cabin next door *alone*, after I rejected his repeated requests for me to join him. It's my first time meeting his parents and I want to make a good impression of a polite, chaste young woman who is perfect for their darling son and wouldn't dare spend the night before we're married.

I smell someone cooking on one of the grills, so I peak my head out the door to investigate. Robbie is two cabins down, in the unit my family has allowed him to live in for the remainder of the off-season, standing in front of the grill in his day-off uniform of a hoodie and sweatpants. He raises his tongs and clicks them a few times in my direction when I wave. Nicole comes into view behind him, emerging from the Grab N Go trail, but he doesn't see her. I don't have time to warn him before she packs a tight snowball and rails him in the back of the head.

"Damn it, Nicole!" he yells, wiping the splattered snow off his shoulders.

"Get used to it, you little shit," she hollers back as she passes him on her way to me.

"Believe it or not, it's a compliment. If she didn't love you, she wouldn't mess with you," I offer as a consolation.

"Lucky me," he muses while turning back around to tend to his grill. I remember showing him how to light a grill just months ago, and now he's cooking breakfast meats on his own. Our little Robbie is growing up.

"Mr. and Mrs. Khaki Pants here yet?"

I step outside and close the door behind me so Nicole can't see how I've stocked and decorated their cabin; I'll never hear the end of it. "They'll be here any minute, so I need your ass to scram."

She holds a hand over her heart, stumbling backward and feigning pain. "Wow, KB, you don't want me here to greet them? That hurts."

"If I had it my way, you'd be at least twenty feet away from them at all times, but unfortunately, you're part of this family now and I have to allow you at Christmas dinner."

She lunges forward to put me in a headlock, but I dodge her grip and hold out my hands. "Don't you even think about it; I need to look good. Don't you have somewhere to be?"

"Yes, actually," she says after another unsuccessful attempt at getting her arm wrapped around me, "Mal and I have a session with Dalia in five minutes, so I don't have time to be messing with your sorry ass anyway."

"How's that going?" I ask, hoping she'll give me something more than the quiet shrugs each time I've asked about their therapy sessions.

"None of your damn business," she says while walking away, but I see the grin on her face as she turns to go.

Twenty-Nine

OUR FAMILY HAS a tradition of opening gifts on Christmas Eve because the next morning is always consumed with the chaos of cooking and packaging up all the takeout meals for the residents of Grady before we close the restaurant at two and have our family dinner. This is how Christmas has been spent for as long as I can remember. We usually hit the eggnog a little too hard, as well, but I see everyone has toned it down in honor of our guests.

It took about five minutes for everyone at Benard's to fall in love with Fred and Jackie Bowen when they arrived in Grady. Fred may not be Nolan's biological father, but you'd never know it by watching the pride in his eyes while he talks about his stepson. Jackie is a younger version of Lily Tomlin, complete with the irresistible smile and contagious laugh. Nolan and I both asked them not to bring gifts, but they didn't want to arrive empty handed, so they brought a tray of homemade cookies, brownies, and bars for the family. Between Nicole and Dougie, the tray is now half empty.

I hesitate to say it out loud because heaven forbid I jinx the bit of good fortune we're having, but if you were to be watching us through one of the giant windows in the family lodge, you'd probably be impressed by the sight. Everyone is laughing, Deb seems to be feeling great, Nolan's family is fitting in like they've known us for years, and Robbie doesn't appear to be bothered at all that he's spending the holidays with us rather than his own family. A buffet of snacks and dips are spread out on the kitchen island, and I'm slowly discovering that the Bowens can handle their liquor as well as the Benards, which only encourages my family to keep the party going.

Nolan and I agreed that we'd exchange gifts tomorrow night in a more private setting, but the rest of us open the small presents we purchased for each other. It's sort of like watching a train wreck in slow motion before it happens—everyone is having such a great time and has a little buzz from the alcohol, but I know when we start opening gifts, it's going to be one of those moments where they realize it's Malorie's first Christmas home and start with the theatrics. My eyes are on the prime suspects—Deb and Brenda. Deb is also convinced this is going to be her last Christmas with us, which I don't believe is true, so emotions have been running high before we even add my long-lost sister into the equation. Sure enough, they slide Malorie a large, wrapped present across the rug from all the aunts, and they start sobbing before the hand off is even complete.

"Ladies, ladies, you need to stop. This is a happy occasion. I'm not opening the gift until you stop crying," Mal says. It's fun to see her tipsy. She just has a look of contentment—no stress, no anxiety, just happiness. That's how I always want to see my sister; though, I wouldn't condone her drinking two and a half cups of eggnog every day of her life.

"Sorry, we just love you and we're so happy you're home. I didn't know that was a crime," Brenda says, wiping her tears with the sleeve of her tacky red Christmas sweater.

I watch Nolan's parents as the scene plays out. I can't imagine how surreal it must feel for them to be immersed in the Benard family for Malorie's first Christmas home. Her face has been seen by every household for the last twenty years, and now she's alive, well, and sitting cross-legged on the floor, arguing with her aunts in front of Fred and Jackie. I wonder what they'll tell their friends when they get home.

"I'm not sure why you handed it to me; the card says it's for both of us," she says, looking at me.

"Go sit next to your sister so we can take a picture of you two while you open it," says Deb, fidgeting with her cell phone to find the camera app. I take it from her hands and get her set up to take the picture before I sit down next to Mal. We pose for a few, and it nearly makes me emotional when I think of how long it's been since we took holiday photos together. I bite my inner cheeks as a distraction while we rip the wrapping paper open with the determination of two twelve-year-olds hoping for the newest Xbox.

It takes both of us reaching across the length of the box to tear the dancing Santa wrapping paper from the top to reveal a complete cookware set for our new cabin. Well, my composure was fun while it lasted. I lose it entirely when it hits me that in the next few weeks I'll be moving into a brand-new cabin with my sister, and we're going to have the best year of our lives, making up for all the lost time. Receiving a set of cookware is a rite of passage she should have experienced when she went off to college. She is nearly forty years old, and this is going to be the first set of pans that belong to her, not her parents or her aunts. I cannot imagine what she's feeling, but seeing me cry sends her over the edge; within minutes everyone in the room is tearing up, including Fred and Jackie.

"I'm so sorry," I tell them. "You must think we're all blubbering lunatics." I pull the neck of my sweatshirt up to wipe my face because the aunts are hogging the tissue box. I can't imagine what my makeup looks like, but I couldn't possibly care less. My sister is home and we're about to start our lives together as a family. This summer is going to be one for the record books.

"Are you kidding me? We couldn't love you guys more, and we're just so honored to bear witness to this beautiful night," Jackie says, wiping her own tears. "I couldn't think of a better family for our Nolan to be spending so much time with. We've been nagging him about not coming home more often, but now I get it."

After having a string of not-so-great experiences with the parents of my partners and not even getting the chance to meet Dave's in person, this is refreshing. Fred and Jackie are kind, loving, and fully approve of our relationship. I steal a glance at Nolan, and he's got a slightly buzzed and euphoric stare, aimed right at me. I might love this man.

"Alright, let me break up the love fest because I have a gift for Malorie, too," Robbie says, surprising us all. He hands her a small, haphazardly wrapped box and says, "I'm so happy I've gotten to know you in the kitchen these last few months, but this spring you promised we are going to work on the dock together, and that's when the real work begins."

Malorie throws her head back in laughter and my heart bursts. My sister is happy. She tentatively opens the box, not sure of what to expect. She lifts the lid to reveal a folded t-shirt and laughs even harder. She holds it up for us all to see: BENARD'S MARINA, SECOND IN COMMAND.

"I'm sure you can guess what mine says," Robbie says with a wink. "First in command."

"Little Robbie, did you finally get a sense of humor? Once you learn to stop over-explaining your jokes, you're going to fit right in," Nicole says, wrapping her arm around his shoulder and clinking the neck of her beer together with his. "Also, I keep reminding you guys this kid is twenty; I'm not sure who keeps buying him beer."

Brenda and Deb suck in a quick gasp while the rest of the room laughs, including Lou.

"You sold it to me yesterday at the Grab and—"

"Shut up, Robbie," she interrupts him. "Cut your losses and move on."

Lou steps outside to smoke, and Fred and Jackie join her, which surprises me because I didn't peg them for smokers. As soon as the door closes, Nolan reopens it and joins them as well. He sure as hell doesn't smoke, so he must need a breather from all the commotion.

"Hey, Chuckie Baby!" Nicole shouts and I turn to see my dad make his entrance into the lodge, wearing a Grinch hat and holding his normal stack of envelopes for us kids. Dad does money, not gifts, which is fine by me. It probably would have been nice to get a toy pony rather than a few crisp twenty-dollar bills when I was in elementary school, but beggars can't be choosers. He chucks the four envelopes at each of us "kids" (including Nicole) as he passes through the living room and toward the patio.

"Merry Christmas to all!" he shouts as he, too, joins the smokers. His addition certainly is testing the capacity of the balcony, but I'm sure Lou is happy to have the company.

I turn to Nicole to make a joke about it when I see her pull her cell phone from the back pocket of her jeans. *Dad* she mouths to me before walking out the door into the back stair-well of the lodge. I've seen her ignore his collect calls from prison a few times, but it's Christmas. I can't blame her for wanting to speak to the only blood relative she still has, regardless of his sins.

"How are you feeling?" I ask Deb as I take a seat on the arm rest of the chair she's occupying.

"Honey, I feel great. This may be the best Christmas Eve

yet," she answers, but I don't believe her. Sure, she looks better than she did last week, but I think it might just be a boost to her system from the magic of the holidays. I've seen her disappear to her room a few times tonight to cough, which sounds like she's literally hacking up a lung.

"Maybe the Ghosts of Grady are going to show us some mercy," I whisper in her ear, nearly falling over in her lap when I lose my balance on the armrest. She shakes her head slowly and lightly squeezes my knee before recovering with a tight smile.

"Maybe," she echoes, but I know she's lying.

The Ghosts of Grady aren't ready to leave just yet.

Thirty

FRED AND JACKIE watch in wonder as our family prepares and serves just shy of two hundred to-go meals before we lock the doors at two and close to the public. The locals think so highly of the Benard family's holiday cooking that some of them have begun making their own meals on Christmas Eve so they can enjoy ours on Christmas or forgo theirs altogether in lieu of our secret-recipe honey baked ham and homemade sides.

Although we're all hurting a little from last night's celebration, we keep the tradition of popping champagne after the last customer leaves, and we lock the doors. Any worry that the Bowens will think we are functioning alcoholics goes out the window as they stand in unison to grab empty glasses for the toast.

"Many years it only took one bottle to fill our glasses. This year, we are surrounded by so many people we love, I'm going to have to open a third bottle. If that isn't wealth, I don't know what is. When you're rich in friends and family, you won't be poor a day in your life," Lou shouts to the dining room.

"To the Benards!" Dad shouts, raising his glass. Everyone matches his gesture and takes a sip while he adds, "I wasn't sure there was going to be a day these broads would let me back in, so cheers to that." A few of us nearly spit out our champagne in response.

"Please give us jobs," Fred says as everyone begins the process of setting up the family dinner place settings.

"We want to feel useful," Jackie adds.

"Please don't let my parents feel useless on Christmas, KB," Nolan says, coming up behind me and wrapping his arms around my waist.

"Oh geez, well, as long as everyone is guilting me—how about Jackie, you help with putting a silverware roll in front of each seat, and Fred, you can help Lou outside on the smoker. If you don't feel like part of the family after getting a good cussing for moving too slow, I don't know what it will take," I say and they both laugh entirely too hard before heading to their assigned duties.

"And me?" Nolan asks, kissing my hand.

"You're being extra sweet today," I say in an accusatory tone. He's always kind, but he's been paying extra attention to me since the moment he and his parents showed up at the restaurant this morning.

"It's Christmas, and I'm in love," he responds, catching the words the minute they leave his mouth. His eyes are wide, and he begins to make mumbled excuses, but I hold the sides of his face in both of my hands to stop him.

"I love you, too, Nolan."

He exhales.

"Thank god. That would have been awkward," he whispers before giving me a soft kiss on the lips, something we've never done in front of onlookers. I'm reminded of this when Dougie yells "Gross!" and Nicole cups her hands around her mouth and begins to boo loudly.

"Ope, I think you have a customer trying to come in," says Jackie, pointing at a figure outside the window. My heart stops when I realize it's Bradford Palmer.

I rush to the side door and push it open before he walks in the snow up to the front entrance. "Bradford, what are you doing here? Are you okay?" I mean, of course he's not okay. His dad and brother are dead, and his mom just entered a guilty plea for aiding and abetting in Lincoln's crimes.

"KB, can we talk?"

"Of course," I say, looking back and motioning to Nolan that I'm stepping out. "Let's go to the lobby of the lodge. We don't have any other cabin guests this week so it should be empty."

Our footsteps crunch in the snow for the duration of our otherwise quiet walk to the lodge. I'm just not sure what to say to him—*How's the family? What's new?* He must feel the same way about me because he remains silent until we get inside the lodge and sit on the overstuffed leather couches in the lounge area.

"My dad's victims are receiving lump-sum payments from his estate," he begins. "One of the lawyers brought over the paperwork to go over it with me, but it's a lot of legal nonsense that I don't comprehend."

"Bradford, with all due respect, there's no way you're going to try and deny restitution for his victims, right?" I ask in the most pleasant tone possible. I'm not trying to fight with anyone on Christmas, let alone a guy who has lost his entire family. I know I'm off base with that accusation because he immediately looks like I slapped him across the face.

"Katie, of course I'm not going to. They can have whatever they want after what they went through. It's just that . . . two new victims came forward."

"That were kidnapped by your dad? Why are they just reporting it now? Sorry . . . that came out wrong. I'm not victim blaming," I say, wishing I could take the words back. I simply mean what kind of story did these girls tell about their absence once they came home? Or were they girls who wouldn't exactly be missed, which seems to describe most of the girls who had unfortunate encounters with Lincoln Palmer.

"They didn't know my dad. They both want restitution for what my brother apparently did to them. Both of them said that Benson assaulted them, putting something in their drinks when they were out. Both girls said they have no memory of what happened leaving the bar, but they each woke up in his bed. They gave the dates and everything. I don't know, KB; it's making me wonder if my dad really did kill him or if it was someone else."

Benson Palmer got a little forceful with me a few times in high school when we had our little forbidden romance, but I assumed he'd grow out of it. He only did it because he was into me, or whatever other lies I told myself about the boy I was so crazy about. I'm yet again struck with guilt over not telling anyone about it; it sounds like I could have saved at least two girls from falling prey to him.

I know Bradford is just looking for anyone else who could have possibly killed his brother so maybe, just maybe, there would be at least one crime his father was falsely accused of. Even if, against all odds, his dad *didn't* kill Benson, he was still a despicable man.

"Who would it have been?" I ask.

"I don't know; maybe one of their dads? Boyfriends? Whoever they told about it? It just didn't make any sense for my dad to kill Benson. He loved him."

"Bradford, it's Christmas. Why don't you come to the restaurant and have dinner with us? We'll have football on, and my dad is making a big batch of spiked holiday punch. We can revisit this once the holidays are over and hopefully get some answers," I say, rubbing his back and quickly realize how patronizing my words must sound. I'm trying to distract him from his anger, like you'd do for a toddler in the middle of a fit.

"Do you ever think about how Grady Lake is this tiny, secluded place in the middle of the woods that nobody had ever even heard of for years? Think of all the time we lived these quiet, normal, happy lives and now it's a nightmare. It's all a fucking nightmare. The people who were supposed to be watching us were the worst ones. My dad, Nicole's dad, Dougie's dad, and now my brother? How is it possible that we all thought this place was untouchable, that nothing bad would ever happen here?"

He's now on his feet, pacing across the hardwood floors in front of me. He's rambling like a mad man, but nothing he's saying is crazy. He's speaking the truth.

Thirty-One

AFTER A FEW MINUTES of calming Bradford down and convincing him that there's nothing we can do about it today, he reluctantly agrees to join us for dinner. When we arrive back at the restaurant, I send him off to fill up ice buckets for the drinks and communicate the situation via whisper to Lou. She simply nods and adds another chair and place setting to the table, as we always do when someone needs a hot meal.

That's the great thing about my family—everyone notices Bradford's presence, but nobody questions why he's here; they simply include him in our plans like he was always invited. The only occurrence that is out of the ordinary is when Lou gives my dad a seat at the head of the table, instead of taking her own spot there. "I'd rather sit by you two love birds and see what you're up to," she says, gesturing to Nolan and me. When I give her a questioning look, she blows out her lips, shakes her head, and pats me on the back before walking away to grab the main attraction—her honey baked ham.

Because our group today is so large, everyone takes their seats and breaks off into individual conversations. Nicole and

Dougie are talking to Bradford about the Packers' playoff chances and their new money-making idea to open a dispensary at the lake; although the city council has thrice struck down the idea of allowing cannabis shops within city limits. Nicole seems to think if the dispensary is *floating* on the lake, the council can't do anything about it, and I don't have the energy to educate her on the thirty reasons why it won't work.

Nolan's stepdad is being incredibly tolerant while my dad goes off on one of his rants about how too many kids have food allergies these days because the genetics are getting "too watered down," whatever the hell that even means. "Send these coddled-ass kids into the jungle for a few tours and they'll forget all about their nut sensitivity," says my father, who did not serve a single day in Vietnam; nor has he any concept of how allergies work. Fred is nodding and giving a curt smile while he politely eats forkfuls of mashed potatoes and squeezes Jackie's knee under the table with his free hand.

I smile while scanning the faces of the unlikely group gathered around me. I spot Malorie and Robbie sitting next to each other. He's telling her stories of working on the dock, detailing each customer's requests and complaints—surely exaggerating a few—and Mal has tears streaming from her eyes while she hangs on his every word. If I didn't know better, I'd think they were siblings with the bond they've formed.

The football game switches over to a halftime performance by a pop star I'm too old to be familiar with (when did that happen?), and the aunts begin clearing plates to make room for dessert. No matter how full you are, *nobody* turns down Christmas desserts made by these three. Brenda likes to tell people that the mayor requested she stop entering her pies into the annual Memorial Day Bake-Off so that someone else would have a chance to win. I'm not sure if it's the truth, but nobody contradicts her while she tells the story.

Once we've all filled our plates with entirely too much sugar, Nolan leans over and tells me he has news.

"The reason my parents and I were talking to your dad and Lou on the balcony last night is because I have something to tell you, and I wanted to run it by them first."

Lou and Dad have stopped their conversations and are watching Nolan with pride. His parents are now holding hands. *Oh, no. No, no, no. I don't want a public proposal. I've told him this.*

"Karli and I have been talking, and we'd love a change of scenery for our home base, and rent in Chicago is getting ridiculous. We found a three-bedroom house just outside of Marquette to rent for the next year. A room for each of us and then a third to make into a studio. It would get us closer to you and Nicole without invading your space too much. What do you think?" Nolan asks, looking across the table to give Nicole a quick wink before turning back to me. She's smiling —*she knew*! "Marquette has all the modern conveniences we could want, including the airport, and we'd have everything we need to produce the show right there in the house. You can move into your cabin with your sister, and I'll make the drive whenever you feel like spending time together. No obligations."

Thank god it wasn't a marriage proposal.

Relieved, I look in Malorie's direction, and she's also giving me a knowing smile.

"Did you seriously run this by everyone before making the decision to tell me about it?" I ask.

"I know how important family is to you, so I had to make sure that everyone was on board. I hope you don't mind."

"And you guys?" I ask his parents.

"We couldn't be happier. We hope to spend a lot of time in northern Michigan next year," Jackie tells me, and I believe her.

"Hell, if this relationship progresses, maybe Nolan will join you all as the next crop of Benards to operate the resort when we hang up our hats," Lou suggests, gesturing to the other two aunts.

"I can't think of a better group to take over," Deb adds, wiping a tear.

I just hope she'll be here to hand over the keys when the time comes.

Thirty-Two

OUR WEEK between Christmas and New Year's is spent like most Americans—in a sugar-induced haze, without wearing real pants unless we need to, and completely unaware of what day it is. The only excitement is that we've been given the go-ahead to start packing up our things for our move to the cabin.

We finally bought Mal a cell phone, under Lou's name of course, and I've been showing her a few harmless apps like Pinterest and Design-a-Room. We've been spending countless hours planning out everything about our new place. I don't think I've felt anticipation like this since we were kids.

Dad is also going to get started on Dougie's new abode, but he'll have to stop when it gets too cold to work, so he most likely won't be moving until spring—something Dougie complains about each time he overhears Mal and me planning for ours.

"Oh hell, kid. You've lasted over thirty-nine years in this lodge; what's a few more months?" Lou asks.

"He just wants something to bitch about, which is why

he's a thirty-something still living with his mother," Nicole quips before Dougie throws up his arms in disgust.

"I get no respect with all these women in the lodge. I wish Nolan would move in so I could have a voice of reason," he tells us.

"Spoiler alert—Nolan thinks you're an idiot, too," Nicole tells him while eating a spoon of peanut butter directly from the jar. This sets in action their typical *Tom and Jerry* routine of chasing each other around the lodge like children. I think the aunts may actually be looking forward to getting rid of us.

I answer a call from Dad, who says that Mal and I need to stop by the cabin sometime this afternoon to check out the paint samples he left for the bedrooms and make a decision on which ones we'd like him to pick up from Sherwin-Williams tomorrow. He also just signed for a package that contains the ceiling lighting fixtures we ordered online, and he needs to know which rooms they belong in. I relay the message to Mal, and she suggests that we head down there now, before the snow intensifies. We aren't expecting anything severe today, just a few hours of thick, fluffy flakes.

We grab our winter coats and slip into our boots before making the three-minute trek to our new home. I can't help but daydream about what it will be like next year at this time. We'll be enjoying the holidays at the restaurant with everyone and then just casually walk home to our own cabin, with our own kitchen and our own bathrooms. What a luxury. I need to thank Dad again for willingly helping the aunts pull off this project for us. Since Mal was given the funds from the donors, she's offered several times to help pay for the cabin, as have I. Each time, Dad and the aunts assure us they've got it covered.

Dad has headed back to Marquette, so the cabin is empty when we arrive. I open the door and let Mal walk in first. When she does, she turns back to me and simply shakes her head. Neither of us can believe it. The overwhelming smell of cedar and fresh paint from the kitchen hits us once the door is closed. Everything is just so new. Yesterday, Dad brought over a small kitchen table and chairs, made by one of his friends in Munising. He used a lot of words I wasn't familiar with, like "epoxy" and "resin," but what I do know is that the table is stunning and features an outline of Michigan's Upper Peninsula in the center, filled with rocks found from the shores of Lake Superior.

We each pull out a chair and take a seat, facing the large dining room window overlooking the lake. The flakes are beginning to get larger, floating over the water.

"It looks like a picture from Pinterest," Mal says, and I'm so unexpectedly charmed that she referenced something she just became familiar with, I nearly cry.

"I could put a picture of it on Pinterest, but nobody would believe us that it's real," I respond, leaning over to put my head on her shoulder. We sit like that for several minutes, just watching the snow. I close my eyes and try to commit this moment to memory because it's perfect. When I'm having a hard day, I want to think of this.

"We are so lucky," she whispers.

There is a light knock on the door of the cabin, and we give each other a knowing smile—it's the first time we've received a visitor in *our* cabin.

"Come in!" I yell and then laugh when my voice echoes in the empty cabin.

Mal and I stay seated but turn to welcome our guest. Sheriff Nelson steps inside the doorway, pulling his hat from the top of his head as he enters and holding it to his chest.

"You're a cop; you're supposed to knock with a little force," Mal says lightheartedly.

We both freeze when we see that Lou is behind him. Her face is the whitest shade of pale I've ever seen.

"What's going on?" I ask as Mal and I both jump to our feet.

"Please, have a seat. We need to talk," Nelson says, turning to close the door behind him and Lou. They both stomp the snow from their boots on the construction mat Dad left by the front door and proceed to join us at the kitchen table, facing Mal and me and the kitchen behind us. I nearly offer to switch so they can see the lake, but I'm not thinking straight.

My last thought before he begins speaking is that whatever horrible news he's about to give us is going to have the most beautiful backdrop in the world. I wish all bad news was given like this, so I'd have something nice to look at while I'm gutted.

"As I told you girls before, I've been isolated from some parts of the investigation into Rich Lowery, Lincoln Palmer, and whatever associates Lincoln had because of my proximity to the case, both real and perceived. I accepted that fate because I knew it was for the best and the agencies who were assigned to get all the evidence would be the best men and women for the job."

We both nod. Lou is staring forward at the table and rocking slightly. What in the hell is he about to tell us?

"At this stage in the investigation, they deemed it safe for me to return to the team in official capacity, which means no evidence is off limits to me. I spent last night, well into this morning, combing through all the boxes they processed from Rich's property."

Next, Sheriff Nelson does something I've never seen him do in my decades of knowing the man.

He loses it.

He begins sobbing so furiously, Lou wraps her arms around her childhood friend and holds him. Malorie and I could not be more confused.

Once he regains composure enough to speak, he keeps

repeating, "I'm so sorry, Malorie. I'm just so sorry. If they let a local look at the evidence, we would have known. We'd have known months ago . . ."

"Known what?" Malorie asks softly.

Nelson doesn't bother wiping his face, he just opens the large manilla envelope he arrived with and produces a document that looks like a sheet of newspaper. It's slightly crumpled but protected behind a plastic cover.

"They didn't think anything of it because they're not from here. They found some newspaper pages in the box with all the trail cam footage and thought he was using it as padding so the footage wouldn't be damaged. They thought it was meaningless."

He turns the article over and slides it in front of Malorie and me. We quickly scan through the words, trying to make sense of why Nelson is so upset by it.

An unidentified baby was left at a safe haven drop off spot in 2004.

He was adopted by Sherri and Robert Stephens.

They named the baby Robert.

Robbie.

2004.

The year Malorie gave birth.

I don't have to turn my head in Malorie's direction to see the movement in her chest. It's rising and falling, slowly at first and then more rapidly as she takes short, labored breaths.

I hear Rich's voice in my head from that jailhouse visit.

You don't need to have a funeral. Just tell Malorie I'm sorry.

"Is . . . is Robbie my child?" Malorie asks Nelson.

"We think so, kid. We think so," Lou says, and nobody speaks for a long time because we're all weeping too feverishly to form words.

6 Months Later

∿

"A DOUBLE WEDDING," Nicole proposes, raising her eyebrows a few times.

"Please leave me alone," I respond, shooing her away. "I've got two hours before my shift, and I want to get some sun."

"Just think about it. Not only would Khaki Pants save money on the wedding, but it would also cut the honeymoon costs in half when we join you."

She gestures with two finger guns before spinning in the sand and heading toward the dock to go harass Mal and Robbie, I'm sure. Ever since she hired someone to manage the Grab N Go, she has entirely too much time on her hands.

Lou is set up in front of the lakeside grill, preparing hot dogs for the annual First Day of Summer party. Every cabin we have is booked, and the best news is that one hundred percent of them are familiar names—returning guests who are kind, respectful, and wouldn't dream of bothering Malorie or any of the other Benards about things that aren't their business. They are only here to get away from their hectic lives for a few days and spend some quality time by the lake. I smile when I see

Lieutenant Barkley get out of his car and make a beeline for Lou, a small bouquet of wildflowers in his hand. It's his third trip to Grady this year, and not one of those trips has been for official police business. I can't think of a better scenario than Lou finding a partner to enjoy life with so close to retirement. She still won't admit that anything is going on between the two of them, but we all have eyes.

I reach back and adjust my beach chair to an upright position so I can watch Mal and Robbie work the docks. Telling Robbie that she might be his mother was probably the scariest and most difficult conversation Mal has ever had to have. It took weeks for the DNA results, but it was a match. Malorie Rose Benard gave birth to Robbie in the spring of 2004. Once he was dropped off by Rich—or possibly Mae, but Rich isn't talking, so we may never know—a full examination was done on the baby, and he was given a clean bill of health before becoming available for adoption. Mal has spoken a few times about what a bittersweet feeling it was to hear that the baby was perfectly healthy after being told he quit breathing immediately after birth, but she's chosen not to dwell on all the *what ifs*. We also may never know why Rich referred to the baby as a girl, but I guess it may have simply been to throw her off the trail in case she ever heard about the adoption on TV and got suspicious.

Telling Robbie's adoptive parents was a complicated situation, as well, especially because they had been basically estranged from their son since his misdemeanor arrest. After the initial shock wore off, they have accepted Malorie as a surrogate member of their family and have worked hard to mend their relationship with Robbie.

As for Mal and Robbie, you couldn't ask for a better outcome—they've become the best of friends. Several times, Robbie has brought old photo albums to the cabin, and they pore over them at the kitchen table so Mal can see what her son looked like at each stage of his life. He was raised as an only child and received all the love and attention Mal could have ever hoped for, in lieu of raising him herself. Robbie also loves to look at old pictures of Mal and spot the similarities in their childhood appearances—the thick, curly brown hair, olive skin, and long, thin fingers.

As for the topic of Robbie's biological father, Lincoln Palmer, Mal answers any questions he has but also relies on a professional to help handle the gravity of it all. Robbie knew Lincoln. Robbie sold him pharmaceutical drugs from the end of our dock. Robbie saw the news when Lincoln was arrested; he knows what the man was capable of. He and Malorie have sat through several sessions with Dalia, and he's begun scheduling sessions on his own to work through it all. The most heartbreaking thing I've ever heard is when Robbie sheepishly asked Mal if she thought any of that evil could live in him and what would happen if it did. "Of course not, Robbie. You are the best of me and your adoptive parents. When I look at you, I see nothing but good," she told him with an arm wrapped around his heaving shoulders.

Once the ground thawed for the season, Nicole paid to have the bunkers removed and destroyed. After months of consideration about what to do with the property now that it's in her name, she landed on the idea of making it into a community park and garden, free for everyone. It's only been open since May, but she's already partnered with several locals —including her once-rivals, the Grady Lake Knitting Club— to create a half-acre garden where everyone works together to tend to the vegetables and various flowers.

The families of Lincoln's victims did not want their names on any sort of plaques or statues, but most of them have visited the land and seemed to enjoy the benches scattered throughout and the newly installed pond in the center of the acreage. Just last week, Nicole added onto the boon dock and installed several boat slips where visitors can park, free of charge, and walk to the Grab N Go, Benard's, or any other business on Grady Lake.

She sold Rich's cabin and the five acres that came with it to a wealthy family from Chicago, who plan to spend their summers there. She knocked down the wall separating Mae's old apartment from hers over the Grab N Go and made it into one giant "bachelorette condo," as she likes to call it. Karli visits often and loves the view of the lake from the balcony off Nicole's room. My dad handled the remodel and took Nicole out for beers at The Moose Trap after each day of work.

Brenda reluctantly helped Dougie furnish his new cabin, after admitting that it was probably time for her baby to leave the nest. She still makes him breakfast at least three times a week and has a spare key to the cabin. If there's a boot in front of the door, that means Dougie had a sleepover—most likely with a tourist or one of the servers from Johnny's—so she simply leaves the breakfast delivery on the patio table outside.

When this tourist season ends, the process of handing off the business to "us kids" officially begins. After a lengthy family meeting, we voted to include Robbie on the paperwork when ownership gets transferred to Dougie, Mal, and me. It's only fitting that he's in line with the next generation to take over Benard's; he's officially one of us.

Lou has retirement plans to drive along old Route 66, surely making detours for some casino gambling along the way. I've heard Barkley mention more than once how much he enjoys a few harmless hands of blackjack, so I think he's angling for an invitation to her little road trip. We all hope he succeeds in getting one.

Although Brenda has mentioned wanting to see the Grand

Canyon and the Florida Keys, I have a feeling she's going to stick close to Dougie and Deb for as long as she can. She's agreed to retire but added that she'll certainly still be making the pies because *who else would know how*? She's made a few comments about how nice it would be to have grandchildren, but I'm not sure that's currently on Dougie's list of priorities.

Deb says she'd like to stay close so she can enjoy watching the kids take over the business her grandparents worked so hard to build, but the truth is that her health is failing and it's getting harder for her to get around. I saw her lean on a fence post to catch her breath for several minutes yesterday after walking from the restaurant to the dock. It wasn't an easy decision, but she's made her mind up—she is going to refuse further chemo and radiation treatments and try her best to enjoy the time she has left with us. Her only wish is that we treat her like we normally would and don't make any special concessions for her; she wants to go out peacefully, surrounded by the same family who has been here her entire life. We are doing our best to comply with her wishes, but its increasingly difficult to ignore her gaunt body and the diminishing light in her eyes.

Nolan and Karli are positively thriving just an hour up the road in Marquette. The new season of their podcast, focused on a missing indigenous woman from Sault Ste. Marie, is shattering the previous records set by last season, when they covered Malorie's case. They are receiving recognition from indigenous tribes all over America for their coverage, and the attention they are bringing to a group who deserves far greater media attention when crimes are committed against their people. Nolan and Karli have fallen in love with the members of the local Chippewa tribe so much, they hired a member to be their official expert for the season. They offered her a cohost role, but she politely declined, wishing to stay behind the scenes and ensure the story of her people is being told accurately and with respect.

The best way to describe my current relationship status with Nolan is easy. Loving him is the easiest thing I do every single day. He always puts me first, but he's not a pushover. He includes Malorie in plans whenever he can and has adorably begun referring to Robbie as his soon-to-be nephew. There's not a day that we don't laugh so hard we cry, and he's even begun calling Nicole "Flannel Shirt" to counter her "Khaki Pants" nickname for him. We aren't yet engaged, but if and when he asks the question, it will be answered with an enthusiastic yes.

Dad started dating a woman in Marquette named Kathleen. We've only met her a handful of times, so I'm not sure how serious it is, but he seems happy and that's all I could ask for. He's cut back on his drinking to a socially acceptable beer or two. I'm not sure if this is her doing or if he just wants to be present for his family, but either way, I'm thankful.

A few tips were called in regarding Chelsey's whereabouts —the callers swear they saw her downstate in Lansing. I can't say I'd be surprised to hear that she is attempting to reconnect with Dave, and I can't promise he wouldn't go for it. He's just another man I thought I knew.

The trail on Uncle Dennis is still cold. If I had my guess, he's still working construction and getting paid in cash under the table. One day, he'll slip up. He'll have to use his real name and identification for something, and he'll be apprehended. At least that's the story I tell myself so I can sleep at night.

Nicole accepts Rich's calls every once in a while, but she hasn't made the journey to southern Michigan to visit him in prison. She tried to talk to him about why he kept Robbie a secret from Malorie, but he changed the subject. It may be a question we'll never get answered.

Bradford has come to visit a handful of times, and I even

spotted him walking aimlessly around the overgrown, vacant property at the former Palmer's Resort when I was out on the boat with Nolan last month. There have been no buyers interested in the now-notorious business owned by Lincoln Palmer, but Mal and I have discussed trying to buy it ourselves. The hardest pill for Bradford to swallow during all of this was learning his brother wasn't the stand-up guy he believed him to be. A total of four women came forward with stories of forced sexual interactions with his brother before the estate was closed, including one the night of his death. He didn't fight any of them on their claims. His relationship with his mother has been understandably strained since her admission, but he does still speak with her occasionally. He's currently planning a move to Duluth, Minnesota, for a job offer he accepted in finance. I'll be happy to see him leave this state and make a name for himself, the honest way.

This winter was pure bliss while Mal and I got settled into our new cabin. We watched movies, baked cookies, braided each other's hair—all the things we missed out on while she was gone. Although she did purchase a preowned Honda Accord from a lot in town, she has yet to spend any more of her donated funds, instead relying on the money she earns working at Benard's. It's a little easier to talk with her about the years she was gone now, and I'm thankful every day that Dalia gave her the tools required to get here. She did confirm her suspicions that her high school friend Taylor was responsible for selling her story and, although they no longer speak, Mal insists that she has forgiven her. Malorie isn't bitter or sad; she's simply determined to make the rest of her life the best of her life. I often catch her outside, staring at the world around her and shaking her head, like she doesn't believe it's real. "We're so lucky to live here," she says to me at least once a week.

The last update, I suppose, is about me. I struggled for a

while, wondering if I was doing "enough" with my life, and then I looked around at my beautiful new house, while surrounded by friends and family who love me, a thriving family resort to manage in a community that feels safe again, and a loving boyfriend right down the road. If this isn't living my best life, I'm not sure what is.

Epilogue

LATE SEPTEMBER

I LEAN FORWARD to wrap the crocheted blanket a little tighter around Deb's legs. "Will you quit fussing? I'm just fine," she lies.

The hospice nurse told us it could be a matter of days now, so we each are soaking in all the time we can with her. Today, she and I are sitting together on the newly constructed dock on the waterfront of Nicole's land. She placed a handful of white rocking chairs out here for the tourists to enjoy the view, but today it's only Deb and me.

We stare out at the calm waters of Grady Lake for a few minutes before she says, "It won't be long now." I don't have to ask her what she means. I remove the extra blanket from my lap and wrap it around her shoulders. She's remarkably coherent today, something the nurses warned us may happen shortly before the end.

"I hope you know how loved you are," I whisper.

"I do," she responds, and we sit in silence once more. A light wind picks up and with it comes a flurry of colorful leaves from the trees that hang over the shoreline. Several ducks glide across the water in front of us as she takes a deep, labored breath and adds, "The Ghosts of Grady are gone now; you know that, right? You can breathe easy, my sweet girl."

"Until Dennis and Chelsey are caught, I'm not sure I'll ever breathe easy, but these last nine months sure have been peaceful. Other than watching my back for her to show up and finish the job of ruining my life, I've learned to let my guard down and enjoy this time in my favorite place."

She stares forward without a word for what feels like an eternity before turning her gaze to me and tightening her eyes slightly, as if deciding what she's going to say to me next.

"I trust you, Katie."

I laugh.

"I trust you, too, Aunt Deb."

"Your Uncle Dennis was not a very good man. He was very abusive to Brenda, and even to Dougie, but I think he was too young to remember. He was very calculated with the abuse—never gave Brenda bruises where we could see them and never laid a finger on her in front of us."

"So, how did you find out?" I ask.

"Do you remember when you came home that summer and he showed up?" she asks.

"Yeah, that's the last time any of us saw him here in Grady. I let Nelson know I haven't talked to him since. Why do you ask?"

"He made the mistake of laying his hands on Brenda in front of Lou. That's a mistake a man will never make twice," she says, raising her eyebrows slightly.

"What, did Lou chase him out of town or something?"

"That's the month we made the last-minute decision to add three more cabins to the resort. Your father was able to pour the cement immediately."

"What do the cabins have to do with—" I stop myself. *Oh my god. Is she insinuating that Lou . . . there's no way.*

"Sheriff Nelson was right, you know. About Chelsey. That's why she was in Grady—to hurt the ones you love the most," Deb says matter-of-factly. "But you don't have to worry about her coming back to finish the job."

"How do you know that?"

"Lou got it out of her."

"But nobody saw Chelsey after we found out she was a criminal. She took off."

"And your Aunt Lou knows these woods better than any law enforcement officer in the state. She wasn't that hard to find."

"She found her? What in the hell did she—"

"We called your dad and got started on a nice cabin for you two girls."

Oh my God. The decision to build us a cabin seemed so sudden, but I just told myself it was Thanksgiving, and the aunts were in a generous mood. *This can't be real.*

"Does Dad know?" I ask, not sure I want to hear the answer.

"Your dad and Lou have had their disagreements over the years, but whenever this family needs him, he shows up. He has kept our skeletons hidden in the closet where they belong. I'm not saying it's easy; I'm sure that's why he enjoys numbing reality with the bottle. But your dad is a good man, Katie."

"So you're telling me that when there is a threat to this family, Lou just 'takes care of them' and buries them on the resort? This sounds like a horror movie. Deb, are you sure you're not just imagining these things? Is this some sort of joke?"

She slowly leans back in her rocking chair, a content grin on her face.

"I remember it all, Katie Bug. And she doesn't always bury them on the resort."

"*There's more*? Who?" I gasp before remembering we are outside and lowering my voice.

"Vigilante is an overused term, but I can't think of a better way to describe Lou. She rights the wrongs, and the world is a better place for it. Katie, sweetheart, I'm asking you to keep these secrets close to your heart, as I have done all these years. I'd hate for my memory to be tainted by being the one to betray my sisters in my final days. Please try to understand that anything Lou has done has been for the good of this family and this community."

I stop rocking and put my hands over the blanket and lightly grasp Deb's boney knees. "Deb, you can trust me. But I need to know who else you are talking about."

"Well, there was the night she found out the apple didn't fall too far from the tree when she overheard that Palmer boy getting a little physical with an out-of-towner."

"Benson Palmer? She is the one who drowned Benson?"

"I'm not saying she killed him herself, but she certainly made sure it got taken care of. A man who puts his hands on a woman isn't something we tolerate at this lake, Katie."

"But they charged Lincoln with that murder."

"I don't think Lou lost any sleep over that, my dear. Nor did she lose any when his fellow prisoners carried out a little jail yard justice."

Holy shit. It was her? She let Nelson get suspended when Lincoln Palmer was beat to death outside his jail. Or did Nelson know about it and let it happen?

"And she let Rich live?"

"Although she reluctantly agreed to it because he's Nicole's father, there was no helping her fury when she found out that Mae knew about Malorie. Mae was supposed to be Lou's friend; she thought of her as a mother figure. Knowing that Mae caused this family so much unnecessary trauma just pushed Lou over the edge."

"I thought I was the only one who knew about Mae's involvement before she died," I point out.

"No, my dear. Malorie broke down and told Lou that night. Made her promise not to tell anyone. Lou never told her what she did, but I'm sure Mal figured it out. She's a smart girl."

"So she forced sleeping pills down her throat so everyone would think she took her own life from the guilt?" I ask, shaking my head in disbelief.

"I'm not sure how she did it, sweetheart. I wasn't there. I just know she came home that night and nodded to me that it was taken care of."

"Sammie?" I ask in a hushed tone, again not sure that I want to hear the answer.

"I'm not sure about that one, Katie Bug. Sammie didn't do anything to hurt anyone else that I know of, so I'd assume the detectives are on the right path naming Chelsey as the suspect. She'll never see the inside of a jail cell, but she's surrounded by cement nonetheless." She shrugs.

I am listening to my aunt—who has been the kindest, most empathetic woman my entire life—casually describe murder in cold blood like she's telling me what kind of sandwich she had for lunch. I know a lot of strange things happen when a person is near death, but she is so calmly and clearly recalling these stories, I feel like I'm talking to a stranger.

"So, I'm just supposed to go on with my life and act like none of this happened? Like there's not a body buried beneath my cabin?" I say, again aware of my volume. "What if she haunts the cabin? What if her spirit wants revenge?"

Deb smiles.

"Well, if she hasn't haunted you yet, I don't think she's going to."

"This is insane. You know that, right? There's been a nationwide manhunt for Dennis and Chelsey, and they've been buried under our cabins the whole time. But people called in reports of seeing Chelsey in Lansing?" I remember the anonymous tips called into the Grady Police Department earlier this year.

In response, Deb shrugs, still wearing the same smile.

"And the texts Dougie gets from Dennis every year on his birthday?"

"What do you want me to say, Katie?"

"This is unreal."

I sit with it for a moment—with all of it. The lies, the murder, the secrets . . . the fact that they did it all to protect this family. Maybe it's not about waiting for the Ghosts of Grady to return. Maybe it's knowing how to handle them when they arrive.

Secret Family Recipes

Beer Battered Cheese Curds
   -1 lb cheese curds (or cubed mild cheddar)
   -1 cup flour
   -1 egg
   -1 cup beer (Lou likes a basic lager)
   -1 tsp baking powder
   -1 tsp table salt
   -oil for frying
*Lou's secret ingredient: one heavy dash of paprika, but you cannot under any circumstances let her know I told you.

1. Heat oil in skillet or fryer to 400°. If you are using a skillet, make sure there is enough oil to cover the curds.
2. Combine flour, baking powder, salt, and paprika in mixing bowl.
3. Add beaten egg and beer, mix until combined. If it's too thick, add another splash of beer. If it's too thin, add a dash of flour.

4. Working in batches, drop cheese curds into the batter and evenly coat and then lift the curds out of the batter with a slotted spoon, letting the excess batter drip off before placing in the oil.
5. Deep fry curds for 1 minute, or until golden brown, then remove the fried curds to drain on paper towels.
6. Let cool slightly and serve.

Benard's Christmas Ham Glaze

*Lou slightly amended this recipe to accommodate the "at home" crowd, rather than preparing in a commercial kitchen.

-1 precooked ham
-1/2 cup orange juice
-4 tbsp butter, softened
-1/3 cup brown sugar
-1 tsp cinnamon
-1/2 tsp allspice
-1 tsp Dijon mustard

1. Score ham with sharp paring knife and place cut side down in slow cooker. Add orange juice to the bottom of pan.
2. In a small bowl, combine remaining ingredients.
3. Using a basting brush, brush ½ of the mixture all over the ham, reserving the remaining ½ for later.
4. Cover, set cooker to low, and cook for 4-6 hours or until internal temperature at the thickest point is 140°.
5. Brush on remaining glaze and cook for an additional 10-15 minutes.
6. Either remove to rest or place under the boiler for a few minutes for a crispier outside – up to personal preference.

7. Slice and enjoy!

Brenda's AWARD WINNING Grasshopper Pie
-15 chocolate sandwich cookies
-3 tbsp butter, melted
-24 large marshmallows (or a 13-oz container of marsh-mallow fluff)
-1/2 cup half-and-half
-2 tbsp crème de menthe liqueur
-2 tbsp crème de cacao liqueur
-1 drop green food coloring
-1 cup heavy whipping cream

1. Place cookies and melted butter in a Ziploc bag and crush them. Brenda says the uppity folks may even have a food processor, but she likes the "humbler" method of crushing them by hand. Press into the bottom and sides of a pie pan, keeping a handful to sprinkle over the top of the pie. Place crust in freezer for 10-15 minutes.
2. In a saucepan, head the marshmallows and half-and-half over low heat, stirring frequently. Once melted, place the saucepan in a bowl of ice to quickly cool. Once cool, add both liqueurs. While Brenda is retrieving the green food coloring to add a drop, Lou usually adds an additional splash of the crème de menthe.
3. In a large bowl, beat the heavy whipping cream until stiff. Pour the cold marshmallow mix into the whipped cream and fold.
4. Pour the filling into the crust and sprinkle reserved cookie crumbs on top. Place the pie in the freezer until firm, at least two hours. Remove 10-15 minutes before serving.

Acknowledgments

While finishing this book, I reached out to readers regarding the ending. I sincerely wanted to know which you'd prefer – a happy ending or a surprise twist. The answer was overwhelmingly "both," which was exactly what I was hoping you'd say.

I've gotten to know and love the Benard Family while creating this series and it felt like saying goodbye to friends. I can't thank the readers enough for encouraging me to write a series – per usual, you were right.

Thank you to my beta readers, ARC readers, and editors (Carly and Erika) for reading my books and giving such great feedback. I smile when I think of how much my circle has grown since publishing my first book.

Brandon, who is the genius behind my book covers and Raven, the soothing voice on my audiobooks, are two people who have sent this series from good to great. I am so lucky to know them both.

Thank you to my friends and family for being my biggest supporters but also giving me just enough shit to forever keep me humble.

Cash, my partner and best friend, thank you for being you.

To the readers: you have shown me kindness and support like I didn't know was possible. Telling your friends, leaving a review, sending me a message to tell me how much you enjoyed one of my books—it all seems too surreal to be my life. I cannot thank you enough for your enthusiasm over my little murder mysteries.

If you'd like to reach out, here are the best ways:
Email: info@jlhyde.com
Instagram: @bookandbeerreview
Snail Mail: PO Box 205, Gladstone, MI 49837